Fiona Thorn
and the
Carapacem Spell

By Jen Barton

D1279593

Table of Contents

1

Every Rose Has its Thorn

"This is a bad idea," Manzy said. "Maybe your worst."

The horse was right, and Fiona knew it. Blowing Jaydin out of prison, especially right under the King's nose, could go bad. Very bad. But only if she got caught, she thought, and that hardly ever happened. McClane had taught her better than that.

"Manzanita Rose," Fiona said, loosening a burr from the back of the horse's neck, "not this again." Sometimes the fact that Manzy was a Bright Eye, a race of creatures known for their intelligence, was annoying. Fiona flung her hands in the cool forest air and flicked the burr to the sky. "No one will get hurt. As long as..."

"As long as they stay out of your way?" Manzy asked, interrupting. She'd set an easy pace for them all morning, taking the dirt paths and familiar trails through the woods, but was now walking so slowly they were almost standing still. She was stalling.

"I know, I've heard it before. But you don't know what you saw. You just think you do."

"I saw an old woman with claws where her hands should've been, Manz. She was covered in ice, and holding a flute," Fiona snapped. "And not just any flute. It was a Sarastro."

"Maybe the reflection wavered funny and you just think you saw..."

"Are you serious?" Fiona cut in, leaning forward. "It was the Moonshadow, not some lily pond. I know what I saw." Fiona huffed and sat back up, nudging Manzy forward with her knees. "Whoever that old hag was, she's the one who cursed the boy, not Jaydin."

Manzy shook her head, her white mane rustling, and walked on. "Some old woman playing an enchanted flute? It doesn't make sense. Only fairies can play Sarastros, you know that. Which is exactly why everyone thinks Jaydin is guilty."

"Just because Jaydin is a fairy doesn't mean he did this," Fiona said, angry all over again. She ducked as they passed under a low hanging branch. "He's never even seen a Sarastro, let alone played one."

"I don't know, Fiona."

"Well I do. Jaydin didn't curse Brent Neulock with a stupid Sarastro or anything else."

"Of course not," Manzy said, stepping carefully over a fallen log, "that's obvious. I mean I don't know about this theory of yours. Or your plan." She snorted, sending a mist of dust floating through the air. She craned around to the left, trying to see the girl. "Honestly Fiona, what's wrong with talking?"

"Like that would work." Fiona shook her head and swatted angrily at a swarm of gnats buzzing by her ear. "One word, Manz. *Chickens.*"

"That was a long time ago," Manzy said. "And this is different." Soft light fell on her hide as she moved, her white fur muted in the speckled sunlight.

"There's no way I'm risking Jaydin's life talking to some old man," Fiona huffed. "Especially one who hates me."

"That old man is still the King. And risking your life isn't any better." Manzanita sighed. "Though it's a bit late for that."

"Whatever," Fiona said, rolling her eyes.

"Fiona Thorn," Manzy hissed, "not everything begins with some sort of explosion."

"It does for me."

Horse and rider continued on the path, heading slowly toward the western edge of the Dappled Forest. Centuries old birch trees flanked them as they rode, their flaking white bark wrapping the trunks that stretched upward. Sunlight poured through the canopy like water from Heaven's own pitcher; little green leaves filtering the bright rays into golden droplets of light and damp patches of shadow.

"I still can't believe you turned to the Moonshadow," Manzy said, irritated. "Looking into the waters without payment takes reckless to a whole new level, even for you." She snuffed loudly through her velvety nose. *"Pay in kind or the winds will still."* She looked around and caught Fiona's eye. *"...the winds will still,* Fiona."

The girl fingered the small bronze key that hung from a chain around her neck. "I know what it means."

Fiona sighed and flopped forward onto Manzy's back. Involving the Moonshadow had been reckless, she knew, desperate even. But with Jaydin's life on the line, she'd had no choice. He'd hang for this, especially if the boy died. She'd needed answers that only The Moonshadow could give. *How do I save Jaydin?* she'd whispered that night, kneeling before the glimmering waters. The wavering image of the clawed hag had appeared immediately. She was the key. She was the one who had cursed Brent Neulock, leaving the little boy in his empty, catatonic state. But why? And who was she? Fiona didn't know, but as soon as Jaydin was free, she intended to find out. She wrapped her arms around Manzy's muscled neck and rubbed softly.

"You worry too much," she said, sitting up. "Caelia trusts me and so should you."

"I'm quite sure Caelia doesn't know that you're planning to blow her son out of prison. Not to mention what you did at the Moonshadow. You're already looking pale, you know that?"

"I am not." She patted Manzy's shoulder. "Relax for once, and trust me. I can handle it."

"Like you handled the hippos?" Manzanita bucked lightly, bumping Fiona into the air.

Fiona smiled, in spite of everything. "They deserved it. It's not my fault they were too dull to understand." She raised her eyebrows. "You act like I hurt them. Which I didn't. I just relocated them."

"They live there, Fee. Hippos are very protective of the water."

"And apparently very dull as well."

"Fee..."

"Were you thirsty or not?" Fiona laughed, leaning forward toward Manzy's head. A persistent twitch of the horse's right flank meant a fly had landed. Not even the flick of her silken tail could shake it loose. "Come on, how good did that water taste after they left?"

"A bit like gunpowder if you really want to know," Manzy said, stopping. They'd reached the edge of the Dappled Forest. There was nothing before them now but the great grassy expanse of the King's Plains.

"What am I going to do with you?" Fiona asked, laughing.

"You could start by getting that fly off my butt."

Fiona lifted one leg up and over, then the other, until she was sitting on Manzanita's back, facing her rear.

"I don't know, Manzy," Fiona teased, "that might be a wolf beetle or even a firebug. Hard to tell. Its bloody fangs are in the way." She laughed and flicked the stubborn fly from Manzy's bottom.

In an instant, everything changed. Manzanita had gone from calm and relaxed to a mass of rigid muscle, rippling with definition and strength.

"Relax already," Fiona said, flipping herself around. "I was just kidding. It was only a meadow fly."

"Hush," Manzy whispered. Her ears were pricked forward, listening. "Something's coming."

Fiona's smile melted as she froze. The King's Plains were known to be dangerous, especially when the summer grasses were high, giving cover to the creatures that lived there.

"What is it?" she asked, "can you tell?"

Fiona's mind raced. They'd seen a few Spotted Cats over the years, glimpsing their speckled hides as the cats scampered from one rocky outcropping to the next. But they preferred the terrain of the foothills to these grassy meadows. Good thing too. A fit horse like Manzy and a girl her size would make a tasty meal for an ambitious Spotted Cat or two. Especially a mated pair working together. *A charred meal at that though*, she thought, remembering her satchel full of explosives. That brought the mischievous smile back to her face.

"Not sure yet," Manzy whispered, shifting her weight from one back foot to the other. Fiona swayed accordingly and without thought, the pair working as one. "Smells too sweet for a Prairie Rat, and it's too clumsy for a snake."

Fiona tilted her head, listening. A heavy rustling of grass floated on the air, bringing the creature closer. "Do you hear voices?"

"Just what I was thinking," Manzy said. "Raiders then?"

Manzanita backed into the protection of the forest as Fiona sunk low and eased her hand into her canvas bag, wrapping her fingers on a block of Blast.

2

A Triple Threat

Isabel was lagging behind. She'd gotten distracted by a small group of Lacewings. The insects had flown out of the tall grass and were fluttering along beside her. Their bright yellows and oranges flickered in the sun as they dipped and flew like paper gliders. Only the Lacewings were better. They never crashed nose first in the dirt. They hovered in midair, each one almost as big as her hand.

The group darted in front of her, with one coming so close he tickled her nose. She smiled and tried to be still, hoping he would land.

"Catch up," Rhiannon yelled over her shoulder, "we're almost there."

At once the Lacewings were gone, melting back into the jungle of grass.

"Thanks a lot, Rhi! He was almost on my nose!"

"Hurry up! The forest is just ahead," Rhiannon said, shaking her head.

****

"Now?" Fiona asked. Her fingers gripped the wad of explosive, waiting for Manzy's signal. One quick squeeze was all she needed to light this place up, Raiders and all.

"Not until they come through."

"Then it's over too fast. Come on, Manz."

"Ssh. They're coming."

"Let's do this," Fiona said, juggling the Blast. The sounds of the approaching riders were louder now and the grass began to rustle in front of them.

"Fiona!" Manzy shouted.

Now we're talking, Fiona thought. She raised the gummy wad above her head and aimed for the rider coming through the grass. "Eat this, Raider scum!"

"Fiona, NOOO!"

Fiona squeezed the Blast, activating the explosive, and understood too late why Manzy had called it off.

Princesses, not Raiders. Stupid, frilly princesses.

She shook her head and threw the wad behind her. It exploded in grand fashion, sending leaves and tiny pieces of bark raining over the forest.

"A bit far from home, aren't you?" Fiona asked irritably as the two riders approached. The oldest rode a chestnut gelding who wore a beaded headstall embroidered with the word, *Prince*.

"Actually, all of Amryn is my home," the first girl said, dusting herself off. "I am Princess Rhiannon and these are my sisters, Isabel and Catelyn."

She was beautiful, despite the dirt and loose bark that had landed in her hair. As she gestured, the wide sleeves of her gown flowed through the air like butterflies caught in a summer breeze.

"We know who you are, Your Highness," Manzy said, dipping her head. "We're pleased to make your acquaintance. And," she added, sinking her head lower, "we apologize for the, umm, explosion."

"What was that anyway?" Isabel cried, shaking behind her horse's neck.

"*That*," Fiona said, "was a waste of perfectly good Blast." Her eyes narrowed as she secretly admired how the youngest, still too small for a mount of her own, rode in a clever pouch attached to Rhiannon's saddle. Below the little girl's head of wispy blonde hair was a wide, mostly toothless grin that spread across her pink, round cheeks. From the neck down the little princess was covered by a frilly dress that puffed from the depths of the pouch in shimmering pastels.

"I haven't seen this much purple satin since the Lady's Moon festival," Fiona smirked, looking at the three of them. She shook her head and laughed. How did they ride in all that foolishness?

"Indeed," Rhiannon said. She wrinkled her nose and rolled her eyes over Fiona, taking in the dusty breeches, the frayed shirt and her worn, leather vest.

Fair enough, Fiona thought, locking Rhiannon in an iron gaze, *but roll your eyes over me like that again, and it's go time, Princess.*

"You almost blew us up!" Isabel shouted.

"Not quite," Fiona said.

Rhiannon stiffened in the saddle and smiled dutifully. "And who are you?"

"I'm Manzanita Rose," Manzy began, eager to change the subject.

"What's that in your bag?" Fiona interrupted, gesturing to the smallest princess. "Some kind of lacy, pet dog?" The child looked to be drowning in ribbons and poof, like she was being swallowed by some kind of cotton candy villain.

"Knock it off!" Isabel whined. Her pudgy face flushed with anger as she picked leaves out of her skirt. "That's our sister."

"Easy, Tizzy," Rhiannon said before turning back to Fiona.

"Don't call me that!" Isabel cried.

"I told you," Rhiannon said, ignoring Isabel, "she's our little sister." She gave Fiona a sly smile. "See for yourself. Her name is Catelyn, but everyone calls her Cricket."

"Some other time," Fiona said. Her patience with these shiny, sparkling girls was coming to an end. She coughed into the back of her hand, trying to ease her scratchy throat.

"She'd love an introduction," Manzy said, bucking Fiona off.

Fiona landed easily on her feet, but was bent over by a sudden coughing fit. She looked at Manzy, her eyes tinged with fear. Manzy stepped forward, but was stilled by Fiona's raised hand.

"Are you alright?" Rhiannon asked.

Fiona took a few slow breaths and stood. "Fine. Just a tickle in my throat." She smiled as if nothing had happened and stepped toward the little girl in the pouch. As she neared, a low rumble could be heard, growing louder with every step Fiona took.

"I believe the royal pet is growling at me," Fiona said, smiling though she was still wheezing a little. Now this was a princess she could respect.

"Just a tickle?" Manzy asked, ignoring Fiona's joke.

"I'm fine," Fiona said. "I just landed wrong."

Cricket opened her mouth, smiling through her threatening greeting. She looked like an alarming little jelly bean.

"I'd rather tangle with a rabid dog than the likes of her," Fiona said, looking at the little girl. She laughed, feeling more her old self again.

"Wise choice," Rhiannon said. She reached down and ruffled Cricket's hair. "Where are you headed? May I see your permit for those...fireworks?"

"A what?" Fiona gasped. The idea that this blue-blooded little brat would even suggest she needed a Writ of Allowance was outrageous. She hadn't carried a permission slip for her explosives in years, not since McClane had cleared her for Angel's Breath on her ninth nameday.

"Our apologies," Manzy said, nudging forward. "It was an accident. And we're headed to the castle, hoping for an audience with your father."

"No," Fiona snarled, "we're NOT. We're just out for a ride."

"We could help," Rhiannon offered, casually tossing her hair over one shoulder.

"We don't want any help," Fiona said, looking at Rhiannon. Aside from the fact that this one had her nose stuck halfway to the moon, the last thing she needed was to add charred princess to her list of violations.

"Actually it's no trouble," Rhiannon said, waving her arm to the side, "royal escort—going once...going twice..."

"I thought we were going to the river," Isabel moaned. "Rhi, you promised!"

"Charmed, I'm sure," Fiona said in her best princess voice. She lifted her pinky finger over her shoulder and walked toward Manzy. "But do go on without us. There's a herd of hippos you absolutely must see."

"Don't mind her," Rhiannon said, glaring at Isabel. "We just pretend she's nine. Actually she still wets the bed."

"Stop it!" Isabel slumped her shoulders and started to cry.

"Actually," Rhiannon said, holding her head a little higher as she smiled at Fiona, "you're now my responsibility."

"Your what?" Fiona laughed. Aside from the small one, these girls didn't look like they could handle brushing their own hair, let alone riding with her and Manzy.

"As Prin*cess*," Rhiannon began, smiling as the word rang in the warm air, "wayward travelers and strangers in need are part of my duties."

"Wayward? Strangers in need?" Fiona shook her head. "What part of NO didn't you *actually* understand?" She should've known. The pompous little twig was just like her father.

Manzy nuzzled her velvety nose into Fiona's chest and whispered, "Put your happy face on. We could use the help." She nuzzled closer. "And maybe the royal healer."

Fiona huffed and hopped up, her stomach fluttering as she realized it had begun. She was beyond the help of a healer now. She'd committed herself at the Moonshadow, she knew that, but it was happening sooner than she'd expected. She rubbed the length of Manzy's soft neck, her hide warm and silky in the summer sun, and hoped she hadn't made a huge mistake.

"It would be an honor to have such a regal escort to the castle," Manzy said.

Fiona looked at Rhiannon and her sisters. "Yeah," she said, rolling her eyes. "Can't wait."

3

Wrapped Tight

"Honestly, Isabel," Rhiannon said as she stood in the barn brushing the dust from Prince, "I thought you were a better rider than that." She laughed and peeked under her horse's neck. "Mother will kill you when she sees your dress."

"Shut up," Isabel said. "It's not my fault that stupid snake came out of the grass and chased a rat under Midnight's feet! You'd of come off too. Being twelve doesn't make you perfect, ya' know." Her face was red and puffed and her badly scratched arms were still bleeding. They were crossed defiantly over her chest.

Fiona was beside her, grumbling and digging through her pack as it rested on a bale of hay. "Do you two ever stop?" she asked irritably. She stepped toward Isabel, opening the small, round tin in her hand. It was filled with a goopy red salve. She was about to rub it on Isabel's arms when the princess screamed and backed away.

"What is THAT? What are you doing?"

"Trying to help you," Fiona said, thinking how lucky the little brat was that she hadn't grabbed something else from her pack.

She took a deep breath and looked at Manzy, wondering how much longer she would force this annoying partnership with the Royal Pains. The

Bright Eye was standing just outside the barn with Cricket. The little girl was picking dandelion greens and clover for her to nibble.

"It's Shadowbell sap, Tizzy," Rhiannon teased as she pulled a metal comb through Prince's tail. "She's trying to poison you."

Isabel's eyes widened. Not an hour ago she'd been thrown into a bed of the strange, poisonous flowers when her horse had spooked on the ride home. As soon as Midnight had seen the snake, he'd bolted from the path. She'd closed her eyes and held on, the sharp blades of grass slicing into her arms the whole time, but she'd wound up on the ground anyway.

She'd seen the beautiful flowers surrounding her right away. They'd been like magic; how they tinkled like little chimes when she ran her hand across the blooms. But deadly magic. And though Manzy had explained they were only poison to eat, Isabel still felt creeped out, like she wanted to keep washing her hands.

"It's thistleberry salve," Fiona said slowly, as if Isabel had been hit with a strong muddling charm, "from the Enchanted Wood. And I'm not standing here with it on my fingers for fun. Do you want it or not?"

"Will it hurt?"

"Only if you keep whining," Fiona said, raising her eyebrows.

"Hurry up, Izzy," Rhiannon said, snapping the lid on her tack box, "We've an appointment with His Majesty, remember?"

"I don't want to see your father," Fiona said as she smeared the salve on Isabel's arms. "And I don't want any more help." There was still a chance she could sneak away from the bickering little darlings and hit the Tower at nightfall. Alone. Accidentally blowing up the King's daughters would not be good.

Isabel twisted away, dragging Fiona from her thoughts. "Stand still or you can do it yourself," she said, grabbing the princess by the wrist.

Isabel stuck her tongue out, but stopped fighting.

"Fiona," Manzy said as she walked into the barn. Cricket followed close behind, her little hands stained green from picking grass. "Do it for Jaydin."

"Jaydin?" Rhiannon asked eagerly. "Is this about the fairy in the Tower?" Her eyes gleamed at the thought of juicy gossip. "I heard he cursed that boy something terrible. They say Brent lays with his eyes open, but sees nothing. That he has no signs of life at all, except for a shallow bit of breath, that the fairy left him empty as any Lecost Bug's shell."

"Some other Jaydin," Fiona said, trying to sound casual. She wiped her hands on her pants and looked away, watching as Cricket tottled to the back of the barn. I wish, she thought. If only your stupid father had found someone else to blame. Then I wouldn't be standing here wasting my time and supplies. And Jaydin wouldn't be wasting away in some cell.

"It is about the fairy who is locked in the Tower," Manzy said sternly. "Our friend, Jaydin, who's held prisoner, just over there." She tossed her head, gesturing toward the tall stone building that loomed in the distance. "And Fiona would be grateful for a chance to prove his innocence."

Fiona glared at Manzanita, hating her for being right.

"Fine," Fiona said finally. She looked at Rhiannon and gestured toward the castle with a flourish. "Lead the way, Fancy Pants."

"Isabel, let's go!" Rhiannon shouted. "Hurry up!"

"I have to get Cricket," Isabel moaned, leading Midnight into his stall, "unless you want to leave her."

"Very funny," Rhiannon said, her hands on her hips.

"I don't know why I always have to do everything," Isabel grumbled as she locked the stall door and reached for a few flakes of hay. She tossed one to Midnight and the other to Rhiannon, who happened to be looking the other way.

"Ahh!" Rhiannon cried as the hay hit her in the back of the head.

"That's what you get for being so bossy!"

Rhiannon stomped her foot and huffed as she picked the loose hay out of her long, black locks. "Let's see what *you* get."

She grabbed a wad of hay and threw it at Isabel. But her sister was already gone, racing toward the back of the barn.

"Children," Rhiannon said, sniffing as she walked toward Fiona, "are *so* immature." She smoothed the front of her rumpled dress with her hands.

"Lighten up, Princess," Fiona said, her fingers caressing the bronze key that hung at her chest, "not everyone has little sisters to spare."

"Actually," Rhiannon began, but was cut off.

~ 13 ~

"AAAAAHHHHH! HELLLPPPP!!!!!

Isabel's cry came from the back corner of the barn, urgent and full of fear.

Manzy looked up from munching on the hay bales and trotted quickly toward her cry, with Fiona and Rhiannon close behind.

"Isabel, what now?" Rhiannon began, but as they skidded to a halt, sending orange dust floating into the air, they saw for themselves.

Cricket was lying on the floor with her back toward them. Wrapped tightly around her small body was a long, black snake. Its coiled muscles rippled as it squeezed tighter and tighter.

4

The Carapacem Spell

"Foster, do you really believe this?" Caelia walked lightly, her delicate feet seeming to float over the soft earth of the Enchanted Wood.

Foster chuckled, his translucent old skin blushing pink with his mirth. "Aye, Caelia," he said, "that I do." She stood tall as any human, and at half her size he had to crane his neck up to see her.

"I don't think it's funny! 'Tis a serious thing you've said this 'eve."

He floated toward her, his nearly transparent wings fluttering behind him. He smiled, looking into the dusky evening sky through a break in the canopy above. "It's not funny lass, not funny at all."

"The why are you PINK?" Her crown of wrapped golden hair threatened to unwind as her thin arms swung beside her in frustration.

Foster hovered beside her, his indulgent smile never faltering. Even the amused look in his eye was constant. Scanning the woods by the trail, he reached out and picked the brightest rosewood blossom he could find. He fluttered behind Caelia and delicately tucked the flower into her lustrous hair. She ignored the gesture.

"Now is not the time for fairy nonsense!" she spat, tearing the bloom loose. "My boy is in danger, Foster, grave danger!"

"Be there any other kind, lass?"

Caelia turned, shooting him a disapproving glare before he could flit away.

"I'm sorry," he said, hovering close to her face. "I came as soon as I was sure." He shrugged his little shoulders. "It's just that with my Shine so close, in these last days of translucence I can't seem to be serious about anything." His smile beamed through his skin, the brightness enveloping him. He giggled softly and flipped in the air, turning somersaults as he traveled beside Caelia.

"Shine or no, Foster," Caelia said, keeping her eyes forward, "you must share this tonight." He flipped gleefully in front of her, like a disruptive child vying for attention. "And by Heaven's Gate, try and be serious!"

It was well into night before all that had gathered to honor the eldest fairy were settled. Foster's time of Shine was fast approaching and the fairies were merry with the thought. It had been a long time since a fairy had reached far enough into their years to Shine; so long that many had never seen it happen. And if his mood was any indication, Foster's burn promised to be brighter than ever, making his absorption by the cosmos a much anticipated event.

"Gather round," Caelia called. She stood alone in front of the large, old oak. Its gnarled branches and twisted, horizontal sprawl served as seating for some of the fairies. They sat in the branches, their delicate wings spread behind them, swinging their glittering legs back and forth.

Caelia brought her palms together and raised her fingertips to her silver lips. A light breeze rustled through the leaves, making her dress sparkle like crystals in the evening glow. She scanned the crowd before her, mostly woodland and field fairies by the look of them, now gathered on the soft moss of the forest floor.

She noticed Eglantina and Gelsae braiding flowers into each other's shimmering hair, and the oldest Tanglefrost boy seemed fascinated by something he'd found in his big toe. Caelia gave thanks to the Angels and considered it a blessing; at least their hands were busy. The smaller flower fairies had stilled themselves finally. Their small glowing bodies hovering in the air were now more like a hundred balls of floating white light, rather than the frenzied blur they'd been earlier.

"As it is Foster's time soon," she began, "I thought we should let him speak first." Amid the uproarious cheering, she gestured toward the old woodland fairy sitting beside her. "I believe he has something most important to say."

Foster stood, and doing his best to ignore the restless fairy who was tickling Shaylee Bramblefly with the thistle bloom he'd finally gotten out of his toe, began to speak.

> *"Know you all how this goes,*
> *Though this one,"* —and he pointed to the Tanglefrost boy—
> *"Has eyes for nothin' save his toes!"*

A hearty laughter rumbled through the fairies, stopping only when Foster raised his hand.

> *"As I fade my senses know,*
> *All that Mother Nature can bestow.*
> *Her every move is clear to me;*
> *The sun in its rise, to the birth of a tree."*

He fluttered his wings, enjoying the attention as he floated above the expectant faces, their eyes alight with the tale. Caelia stood by the oak, her wings twitching in irritation as she waited for him to get on with it.

> *"But to me came a heavy care,*
> *As darkened magic filled the air."*

He swept his hand in a half circle and flew forward. The fairies in the front row leaned back, their eyes and mouths wide open.

"'Tis no dark magic in the land!" a yarrow sprite chimed, gliding down from above. "His final jest is mighty grand!" she squeaked, a tiny speck of light flitting with jubilation.

The fairies sighed with relief and began giggling.

"Enough!" Caelia's command was undeniable. The little yarrow sprite zipped behind the trunk of the tree so fast she looked like a tiny shooting star. Even the Tanglefrost boy stopped fidgeting when Caelia glided to the front, spreading her large purple wings and hovering above the ground.

"'Tis no jest. What Foster said is true." She glanced at the old fairy, now sitting in the front row, a sheepish smile on his face. "His intuition is high. May we all be so lucky, to reach our final translucence." She noticed many fairies nodding in agreement. Speaking of the glorious time of Shine was like a balm to her shattered nerves.

"On the day the young human was attacked, Foster sensed dark magic rippling through the air, spreading from the Bitter Mountains."

The fairies were aghast. Eyes wide and full of fright, they listened as Caelia explained.

"Though most of you are too young to know, magic this powerful leaves a mark. A mark undetectable to all but the most aware, the most connected to Our Mother, the old translucent ones."

Foster stood and faced them. He raised a hand in salute, acknowledging his honored status. The fairies laughed, even Caelia smirked at his insolence.

"He suspects the boy was a victim of old magic, of something called the Carapacem Spell."

A shiver swept through the crowd, their light hearts unable to hear such vile words without cringing.

A smart lad in the back shouted, "But ma'am, are you saying the Guardian cursed the boy?"

The crowd gasped. The yarrow sprite peeked from behind the trunk and squeaked, "Uh oh...," before flitting for cover.

"Certainly not!" Caelia lost her patience as Jaydin's honor was questioned.

She inhaled deeply. The night forest surrounded her; the dark earth, damp and musky, the spicy sweetness of night blooming jasmine, the clean freshness of new rain glistening on tiny tongues of lush ferns. She was their Queen as well as Jaydin's mother; Caelia Rowan, a former Guardian herself. The lad meant no harm. It had been a question and nothing more.

"Jaydin was a vehicle for the magic. We think the spell was meant to go through him to the boy. What we don't know is why."

Sebille Shimmerfrost sat above Caelia, the fabric of her orange skirt dangling above the Queen's head. Her short auburn hair framed a face of such innocence that she was often the surprised victim of some of the more mischievous fairies' pranks. When she spoke her voice was so soft it was only by virtue of her position that Caelia heard her at all.

"But ma'am, who would do such a thing?"

Caelia looked up, searching for the gentle voice. She found Sebille, saw the honest question in her eyes. She hovered until she floated in front of the little sunflower fairy. Cupping Sebille's face in her hand, Caelia looked into her trusting brown eyes.

"Who indeed, child? Who indeed?"

5

For the Love of Lindley

Choosing the plumpest baby was always her favorite part. She smiled and lifted the best one from a wriggling clump of hatchlings gathered in the corner.

"That's it, my love," she whispered, clacking the rusting tips of her claws together. "It's time."

She pinched the baby's black abdomen and brought it close to her face for inspection, nodding in satisfaction. She smiled and the sheet of ice that coated her skin cracked, sending small chips falling to the floor in a jagged, tinkling flurry.

A larger adult spider scurried out of her way as she shuffled past, its prickly legs almost catching on the old woman's tattered skirts. It scrambled behind a block of dirty ice that had been molded into a chair and tipped over an empty cauldron. The metal pot clang dully as it cracked the icy floor below. The spider settled behind the chair and watched, peering from behind as once again one of its own was chosen.

"Calm down, Persephone," the hag said, still admiring the young arachnid. It was dangling from a gossamer thread attached to one of her thick, iron nails. "There are always more."

Persephone watched, her eyes blazing with fury. The hag chuckled, then gathered the dangling baby into her palm and crossed the cave to her cauldron.

The liquid within was thick and still; mirror-like in appearance. As the old hag leaned over, her reflection flickered before her. *This is their fault as well,* she thought, seeing what these years in the mountains had cost her. Dirty hair clumped in thick mats around her face and ears, falling onto her shoulders and around her face. She reached up to feel the wrinkled, graying skin of her once blushing cheek, but as ever, the wretched film of ice that had grown fast to her skin prevented even the warmth of her own touch.

She sensed Persephone slipping from behind the chair, silently crawling forward, her eyes focused on her young. When she caught the stinging scent of Persephone's venom, she laughed.

She thrust the baby out, holding it above the silver liquid. It wriggled furiously in her slippery, metal claw. His whiskery legs stuck out in all directions, running through the air, desperate for escape.

"I wouldn't, my love," the hag warned, her voice calm and even, the threat cold as her icy lair. Persephone hunched behind her, frozen in fear even as the deadly venom dripped from her fangs, melting holes in the floor below, even as her blood boiled with hatred, even as one of her own was chosen.

The hag opened her iron claw and the baby plopped into the cauldron. For a second he held himself on the surface, his tiny eyes wide with terror, then sank into the thick liquid below. Heavy, shimmering waves rippled from the center, rolling out to the sides before disappearing. Persephone shrieked, a piercing scream that shattered ice in all directions, sending a shower of crystals flying about the cave.

The hag closed her eyes as icy bits flew through the air, bouncing off the cauldron and the walls. Her iron hands gripped the curved edge of the cauldron and she began to whisper.

"Now show me. Show me what I want to see."

The rolling silver stilled. The surface became smooth and hard and flashed bright white, shining up into her face, making her wrinkled and twisted features seem to glow with power. The blinding light blinked out, replaced by the flickering scenes that played for her alone.

Large green wings fluttered uselessly back and forth as a handsome young fairy tried in vain to hover in his tiny cell.

The liquid shimmered briefly, then hardened again.

A muscular man, sweaty in the summer heat, was building something large and wooden outside.

But what was this?

She smiled as the realization came to her, disturbing the crust of ice that coated her skin. A gallows. He was building a gallows for the fairy.

Plink! Plink!

Drops of water bounced on the hard surface as it flickered with more scenes. The heat from the cauldron was melting the icy chips that fell from her face. Her smile was growing.

The silver shimmered again, then hardened.

Now it was her, with her beloved Sarastro that day at the Rowan Oak. She watched herself standing beside the fairy as he played for the boy. He'd had no idea. No one did. Her plan had been perfect.

Plink! Plink! Plink!

She reached to her mouth and found her skin almost bare. Her smile had melted the crust from around her lips. She turned back to the cauldron, eager for more.

The liquid shimmered, hardening once again.

A large tree stood on a grassy hilltop. It was familiar, somehow, like the soft, blurry edge of a memory.

What is this?

Two fairies sat in the tree, their legs dangling from the bottom branch of the old maple. Their wings were closed behind them, and they were holding hands.

To be so young and beautiful!

Her smile widened to see the youthful lovers, but was lost as the realization hit her. She gripped the metal edge of the cauldron tighter and drew a sharp breath.

It was them. The two who had betrayed her.

They'd been paying so much attention to each other, with their whispering and laughter, they hadn't even heard her coming.

She fought to look away from the vision, to look away from the old pain. But she couldn't tear herself from the memory of Lindley. She was frozen.

She stood beside the cauldron, her body beginning to shake with fury.

How they'd begged for her forgiveness. That would be nothing compared to how they'd beg this time.

She flung her head back and screamed furiously. The shrill, piercing scream sent Persephone's young ones scattering about the cave in all directions, running for cover from this strange cry of anguish.

The hag's twisted claws flew to her mouth to keep the pain buried, where it belonged. And this time she felt nothing but the chill of hardening ice. The crust was creeping over her skin again, freezing her with its bitter cold.

This was not what she had wanted to see.

6

Kevin

"Do something!" Isabel screamed.

Manzanita bared her teeth, the whites of her eyes flashing through the haze of barn dust, and reached for the snake.

Fiona reached for her pack, but realized she'd left it on the hay bales.

Isabel hid her face in her hands. "I can't watch, I can't watch!"

Manzy was closing in, but as she neared the coiled muscle that was wrapped around the little princess, Cricket sat up. The snake let go and slithered to the floor.

Isabel scooped her sister away from the retreating serpent. "Cricket! BABY! Are you okay?"

Rhiannon fussed and ran her hand through Cricket's hair. "Master Lyons will hear of this! Snakes in the barn!" She steamed and shook her head. "What's next? Filthy rodents?"

"Achoo!"

"Bess you!" Cricket giggled.

Manzanita stood her ground, watching as the snake slithered through the saddles on the floor, trying to find a place to hide. "Get back, girls," she warned.

"Achoo!"

"Bess you!" Cricket giggled again. Then she squirmed and fussed and twisted and rutched until she'd freed herself from her sister. She slid down and landed on her bottom in the dirt, her dress fluffing around her. She crawled to her feet and ran as fast as she could toward the saddles. "AKE!!!" she said, bouncing up and down in front of Manzy. "AKE! AKE!"

"IT'S BACK!!!!" Isabel screamed, pointing to the floor.

Rhiannon tried to snatch Cricket, but missed. The little girl was headed straight to where the snake was poking its head out from under a saddle.

"Kevin?" Fiona said, her eyes narrowing as she saw the snake's head for the first time.

"Fiona? Is that you? Manzanita Rose?" a cheerful voice asked. "Achoo!"

Manzy relaxed, realizing that the snake was totally harmless; an old friend in fact.

Cricket bounced up and down, pointing and shouting, "Bess you, Ake! Bess you!" She held her foot out and the snake began to slither up and around her little body.

Isabel and Rhiannon scrambled forward, lunging for their sister.

"Girls, girls," Manzy said, catching them with her neck, "it's alright."

"You spoil everything, Manz," Fiona said. "That was about to be a three princess pile up, head first in the dirt."

"I'd like to introduce Charles Ebeneezer Fitzpatrick the Third," Manzy said, gesturing toward the snake with a toss of her head.

"But my friends call me Kevin," he said, easing down from Cricket's grip long enough for introductions. "Pleased to meet you."

Kevin slithered over the dusty floor toward Isabel. The princess stepped back and screamed.

"By the Angels child! Thanks be I have no ears!" he began. "I'd wager you could loose blood from a stone with the blistering level of your caterwauling!"

Isabel looked at Manzy, her fear lost in the tumbled mish-mash of Kevin's words. "Huh?"

"You're loud," Fiona answered.

"Oh."

"Is this some kind of trick?" Rhiannon asked, nudging forward. "Who are you? Why exactly were you squeezing her so hard?" She glared at him. "Do you know who I am?"

"Hey, Kevin," Fiona interrupted, raising a hand in salute and rolling her eyes at Rhiannon. "Welcome to my nightmare."

"Fiona," Kevin said, nodding in greeting. His body lay stretched in front of Manzy. Only the end of his tail remained with Cricket. She sat on the ground laughing, mesmerized by the way he kept flicking the tip of it gently under her nose.

"I was comforting her, Princess," Kevin said, laughing. "She was sad to hear you and your sister fighting so. It was a hug you saw, I assure you." He glanced at Manzy, to be sure she understood as well.

"Your eyes are weird," Isabel said, twisting back and forth where she stood. "You don't look like other snakes...sir," she added, remembering her manners at the last minute.

Kevin raised himself a few inches, cocked his head to the side and glanced at the girls. His black eyes, which were shot through with a yellowish-gold vertical slit, looked at them through a lush pair of long eyelashes.

"I'm not like other snakes," he said proudly. "I'm a Sneezing Snake."

"A what?" Isabel asked, raising her eyebrows.

"He's a Bright Eye," Fiona said, "like me and Manzy."

"Actually," Rhiannon said, sticking her finger in Fiona's chest, "*you* can't be a Bright Eye. You're human, just like us." She smiled smugly.

"First of all," Fiona said, wrapping her hand around Rhiannon's finger and curling it back into the girl's palm, "I'm nothing like *you*. And most importantly, I've been an actual Bright Eye for thirteen actual years, regardless of what you *actually* think."

Rhiannon huffed, then slid to the other side of the barn, rubbing her fingers in her hands.

"Is that why you were sneezing?" Isabel asked Kevin, oblivious to the tension between her sister and Fiona. "Or do you have a cold like Fiona?"

"I don't have a cold," Fiona snapped.

"Usually, dear," Kevin explained, "I only sneeze when I'm nervous. Which I was." He shivered, remembering how Manzy had almost bitten him in two. "But the dust in here is quite dreadful."

He settled on the ground and sneezed again. His body tightened, shooting out flat as a board as the powerful spasm overtook him. "See what I mean?"

Cricket squealed in delight. "Bess you, Ake! Bess you!"

"Doesn't that hurt?" Rhiannon asked. She scrunched her face in disgust.

"The unique elasticity found in the majority of my vertebra (achoo!) enables the movement to occur (achoo!) without significant discomfort."

"Bess you," Cricket giggled again.

"Did you get all that?" Fiona asked, raising her eyebrows at Rhiannon. The girl's head was so cluttered with pronouncements and theories there was likely no room for much else.

"Yes, of course," Rhiannon smirked.

"Well, I didn't," Isabel said.

"He says it doesn't hurt," Manzy explained.

"Kevin," Fiona said, "what are you doing here?"

"I am on assignment." He proudly raised himself a bit higher. "A direct result of my employment in the secret service of our Eminence, the honorable Lady Dax."

Manzanita could feel the question on Isabel's face before she even turned around. "He's a spy for our leader."

"Ahhh, okay," Isabel said with a content smile.

"What assignment, Kevin?" Manzy asked seriously.

Kevin's eyes flashed behind his thick lashes. "We have information," he began, nervously glancing at the princesses, "that the fairy isn't the only one in, shall we say, jeopardy."

7

The Spy Who Loved Me

The sun had begun to set, its reddish glow spreading from a bright hot center on the horizon like an egg of fire cracked in the evening sky. Streaks of pink rippled through the dusk, reaching over the darkening blue of the ocean as Kevin and the girls headed toward the castle.

Manzanita stood outside the barn, watching them go. Her mind echoed with the threatening shouts they'd heard earlier in the afternoon as they'd entered the village and ridden by the Great Stairs. A crowd of villagers had been gathered, chanting for the death of one of the kindest boys she'd ever known. Brave, too. Not even Fiona had managed to drive him away.

A chill ran over her white coat.

Hold on, Jaydin. Just hold on.

****

"I don't see what the big rush is about," Isabel said as they approached the castle. She and Rhiannon walked the dirt cart path that led to the castle, with

Cricket bouncing beside. Kevin trailed along in the grass and Fiona followed behind.

"Just an innocent life," Fiona said. "But don't trouble yourself."

"How could he be innocent?" Rhiannon asked, without turning around. "Everyone knows he cursed the boy with the Sarastro. The only reason he hasn't been hanged yet is because Father wants to find out why."

Fiona raised her fist behind Rhiannon's head and drew back. Knocking the lie out of her mouth might be worth spending her life in chains.

"And because Uncle Ferront thinks he's innocent," Isabel said, skipping lightly on the path.

"What?" Fiona said, dropping her fist.

"What did you say?" Rhiannon asked, grabbing Isabel by the arm.

"I heard him arguing with Counselor Graven this morning," she said, shrugging away from her sister. "He doesn't believe it was the fairy." She smiled at Fiona. "And he's trying to convince Dad."

"Perfectly sensible," Kevin said. He looked up at Rhiannon and smiled. "Sarastros are quite rare, and their magic is not easy to master. It's simply not logical that a fairy of Jaydin's age could perform the deed of which he is accused."

"But the Guardian is one of the most gifted musicians in Amryn," Rhiannon said. "I bet he could play any instrument."

"It is not so much about the playing, child," Kevin answered. "but about the migration."

"Huh?" Isabel asked, squinting at Kevin.

"Yeah," Rhiannon asked, scrunching her face, "what do you mean *migration?*"

"Sarastros are more than simple enchanted flutes. They are imbued with complex magic that allows the user to become one with the instrument; to bind the very soul of the musician to the flute itself."

"So," Rhiannon said slowly as Kevin's words sunk in, "you're saying he couldn't do it? That it's actually impossible for the fairy to be guilty?" She looked from Kevin to Fiona, a smile spreading across her face. "We have to tell my Father!"

Fiona patted her on the shoulder and laughed. "That's the smartest thing you've said all day."

Ahead two men busied themselves with the nightly chore of lighting the sconces on either side of The Great Stairs. The angry crowd from the afternoon had dwindled to a handful of villagers. They seemed less boisterous now, more interested in warming themselves by the sun's heat that had baked into the stone steps than in vigilante justice.

"You and I should go first," Rhiannon said, gesturing to Fiona. "If we all go together it might draw too much attention."

Fiona nodded, surprised at the sense in the girl's plan. Perhaps there was more to her than shimmering satin and poofy skirts after all.

"Unless you don't feel up to it," Rhiannon said, looking Fiona up and down. "You look awful."

"I'm fine," Fiona growled. So much for the girl being sensible. "And stop looking at me like that. I swear, do it again and I won't be held responsible."

The two walked off, heading toward the Stairs, Rhiannon stomping along as Fiona shook her head.

"Why didn't Manzy come?" Isabel asked Kevin as she watched the older girls go.

"No need," Kevin said. "I'll just have a quick look around the castle and we'll rendezvous back at the barn." He lifted his head just above the grass, scanning for other villagers. "Princess, are you quite ready? Our proximity is most favorable."

Isabel looked at him blankly. "Huh?"

"I believe we are close enough now." He looked expectantly from under his long, dark eyelashes.

"Do I have to?"

"We did agree this was the best way," Kevin said, slithering closer.

Isabel stood with Cricket, looking at Kevin. She was getting used to him. She was even starting to like him. Earlier, when she'd seen him sliding along beside them she thought how pretty he was, like a shiny black ribbon twisting smoothly through the green and brown grass.

But this was too much.

"Why can't you hide under Cricket's dress?" Isabel asked. "She'd love it. Just look at her."

Cricket stood beside him, holding her skirt above her head in an invitation.

"You know I wouldn't fit. I'm too big." Kevin laughed, shaking his head at Cricket. "Come now, I'm as harmless as could be. I wouldn't hurt you, I promise."

"It's not that," Isabel said. She scrunched her face and confessed, "It's just that you'll be all...slimy."

"Ah ha!" Kevin said, "I'm not slimy! Touch my scales and see for yourself."

He arched into a taut curve and Isabel ran her fingers over his shining scales. To her surprise they were dry, and more delicate than she imagined.

"Okay," she said, eager to be such a big part of the plan. "I'll do it!"

"Ahh, there's a good girl!" Kevin said, smiling. "I'll just climb up and then wrap around your waist."

Isabel watched nervously as Kevin began to disappear under her skirt. She squeezed her eyes shut and stood still. But there was just no helping it; not even Cricket bouncing up and down and laughing could help her relax.

But then the funniest thing happened. As Kevin inched up the outside of her leg, she laughed. She felt each scale grip her leg, then her middle, like a hundred little fingers tickling her at the same time. She hopped from one foot to the other, trying to control herself.

"Princess?" Kevin called shakily from under her dress, "Achoo! You're not making this any easier, dear. Achoo!"

"Sorry!"

Isabel laughed, trying to stand still. And although she looked like she'd just eaten the biggest meal of her life, the plan seemed to be working.

"Izzy! AKE!" Cricket shouted, laughing and pointing to Isabel's middle.

"Yes baby, I know. Ake."

"All set out there?" Kevin asked.

"I think so, okay in there?"

"Nice and cozy. Let's go."

They walked up the Stairs and passed through the main hall without attracting any attention, then headed for the King's chambers. The stone passage was lit by sconces, and Isabel slowed, mesmerized as always by the etchings on the chamber doors.

Each was marked with the unique, intricately carved design belonging to the counselor who worked within. On the first door to the right a grand stallion was depicted. His head was lifted, the full mane flowing in a timeless breeze as he listened to the perpetual whispering of a hummingbird that floated beside his ear.

"Are we there?" Kevin whispered.

"Not yet," Isabel said. "I just slowed down to look at the doors. They're so pretty."

Kevin wriggled his head up through the neck of Isabel's dress and looked around the hallway. "I see what you mean."

"This is Uncle Ferront's chambers," Isabel said confidently. "The stallion stands for nobility and grace."

"What does the bird say to him?" Kevin asked, enchanted by the carving.

Isabel looked toward the ceiling and squinted her eyes. "The hummingbird whispers of dreams, I think." She looked down, trying to see Kevin as he stuck out of her dress. "It's hard to remember though. We study them in lessons with Master Laird."

"What about that one?" Kevin asked, looking across the hall. Its carving was as beautiful as the first, though completely different.

"That's easy," Isabel said, walking to the door. "It's Counselor Graven's. I got in trouble because I said he looked like that ugly bird. I had to help Mistress Brandywine clean out the trash bins that night after dinner. So gross!"

On Graven's door was a giant vulture with its wings tucked back, perching on a piece of driftwood. The bird's long, wrinkled neck reached down, stretching from its feathered collar. The sharp beak was open, bent toward a small frog it held beneath its talons.

"I don't remember what it's supposed to mean," Isabel said, laughing as she remembered all the greasy potato peels that had ended up in her hair. "I think the vulture is patient, or something like that. I forget about the frog."

"Frogs are symbolic of opportunity," Kevin said.

"Come on!" Isabel said, running the rest of the way down the hall with Cricket trailing behind, "I want to show you my favorite one!"

Kevin ducked down and gripped tightly, bouncing along as the princesses raced through the hall.

"This is daddy's room," Isabel said. "His door is the best."

Kevin popped up to investigate. The carving showed a large bear standing on all fours, its eyes gazing out from a massive head. Perched on the bear's shoulders was an eagle. The regal bird looked into the distance while its talons gripped tightly, leaving small runnels of what could only be blood flowing into the bear's thick coat of fur.

"Judgement and freedom rest on the shoulders of bravery and powerful benevolence," Kevin recited from memory, awestruck by the powerful carving. "The creed of the King. Of course."

"I just love the eagle," Isabel said. "I wish I could fly." She shrugged her shoulders and knocked on the door. Kevin ducked below.

"Hang on! Hang on! I'm coming." It was Rhiannon.

A bolt slid back on the other side, the heavy metal clinked into place, and Rhiannon opened the door. Fiona was on the far side of the room, pacing in front of the large windows that looked out to the sea.

"Where have you guys been?" Rhiannon scolded. "We've been waiting forever."

Cricket ran in first and began spinning circles around the leather chairs in front of the King's desk.

"Nowhere," Isabel said. "Where's Dad? Did Fiona get to see him?"

"He wasn't here," Rhiannon said impatiently. "But she had another one of those fits." She looked at Fiona and shook her head. "I think we should get Mistress Nan."

"We don't have time," Fiona said. "I'm fine." Besides, there was nothing their Mistress could do.

"I was just about to leave a note for Father," Rhiannon said to Isabel, "when you knocked." She walked back to the desk, picked up her quill and began finishing her note to the King.

"All clear," Isabel said, peeking down the neck of her dress.

Kevin slid to the stone floor and moved toward Cricket. At the sight of him, the little girl's face lit up and she bounded across the room.

"AKE! AKE!" she cried, her small hands reaching for Kevin. She plopped down and began playing with his tail.

Rhiannon shook her head. "How did your first adventure in espionage go, Izzy?"

"Huh?"

"Delightful," Kevin said. "Isabel was a natural."

Fiona stopped pacing and looked at Kevin. He was wrapped around Cricket, the fluffy lace of her dress squishing between the rings of his body like icing on a cake.

"Did you see the King on your way?" Fiona asked.

"No," Kevin said.

"We can't find him either," Rhiannon said. She held up the note. "But I left him this. When he sees it, he'll find us. Guaranteed." She looked at Fiona and shrugged her shoulders. "It's just going to have to be good enough for now."

"Well it isn't good enough!" Fiona shouted, angry at the casual dismissal.

She strode to the door, frustrated with their lack of progress. What had she been thinking? Parading around the castle with Princesses. As if the King would actually help her anyway. She grabbed the doorknob and turned toward the others, her smile determined and dangerous. "Just forget it."

"Fiona, wait!" Rhiannon called.

But it was too late. She was done listening to pretty princesses and waiting for a useless audience with His Majesty. She was done with partnerships and teamwork. But most of all she was done doing nothing, feeling helpless as Jaydin's days ran out, one after the other, locked in a stinking stone tower.

"I'll do it myself," she said bitterly. Jaydin didn't have time for this. And neither did she.

But as her hand began to turn the knob, something felt strange. There was pressure on the other side.

Someone was out there.

Fiona's head snapped around, her eyes wide with surprise. She shook her head, then raised a finger to her lips motioning that someone was on the other side, talking.

Rhiannon snuck over and leaned against the door, listening. Isabel stood by the desk, holding her hands over her mouth.

Kevin slithered to the door and settled, wrapping himself protectively around Cricket. This was exactly what he'd come for.

Fiona focused on the voices, but her heartbeat was loud in her ears, and for a second all she heard was her own blood rushing through her veins.

THUMP! WHOOSH! THUMP! WHOOSH! THUMP! WHOOSH!

"...and all of it is his fault," said an old man's voice, breaking through the rushing noise in her head. "The King's time is due. Overdue." The voice was silky and smooth, like polished poison.

"But what will you do, sir?" another man said, his voice deep and husky.

"Nothin' else he can do, is there, huh?" This time the voice was shrill and squeaky; a third man on the other side of the door.

"Shut it, will ya? Was I talkin' to you?" the deep husky one said.

"Patience has been mine," said the silky voice again, "and now it's time to rid ourselves of both of them. The King and the filthy fairy."

The girls exchanged fearful looks. Fiona's eyes narrowed, surprised by this new treachery.

"See! I told ya," the husky one said, slamming a meaty fist into the other.

"Perhaps the Tower guard could become ill," the old one said. "and then you two can finish the fairy." He laughed quietly, a thick, evil sound. "I'll take care of the other. Personally."

Fiona's jaw clenched as she battled the fury building within. No one was going to finish Jaydin, at least not while she was around.

Rhiannon's head spun, trying to make sense of the sudden threat to her father, while Isabel huddled fearfully by the desk.

Cricket sat quietly behind them with Kevin wrapped around her.

And she *was* quiet, for awhile. But then she began to growl.

After that, everything happened at once. The growling got louder, Kevin got nervous, and...

"Achoo!"

Fiona fought the pressure building on the door handle, but it was no use.

The door swung open.

The girls fell back, scattered in a heap. Standing in the doorway, a crooked smile parting his thin lips, was Counselor Graven. A long, black cloak masked his bony frame, and though he was old, his eyes held nothing of age or weariness. They were, in fact, very alive with the excitement of his new discovery.

To his left stood a tall man with lanky arms and ugly green teeth above a pointed, whiskery chin. His watery eyes flicked nervously back and forth from the girls to Graven.

On the right stood a shorter man of younger years. His beady eyes, placed a little too close together, glistened with an eagerness for his job. He quickly assessed the situation and began pounding a meaty fist into his palm, awaiting instruction.

"Get them," Graven said, never taking his eyes from the girls. He absently twisted the gold ring on his finger. "And then bring them to me."

He turned and left, confident his orders would be carried out. His cloak trailed behind him like a black cloud, leaving only his words hanging in the air like a poisonous vapor.

8

Jaydin

It was hot. Too hot. He sat on the floor with his wings spread behind him, pressed against the curved wall, hoping to pull some chill from the stone. But it was useless. His tiny cell had only one small window. Any air that did bother to come in was heavy and thick, nothing like his fresh, cool home in the Wood.

And so today would be just like the rest. Like every other day for the past two turns had been; sitting, pacing, dealing with the constant sweating. Not to mention listening to the crowds clambering for his death as they stomped about below. There wasn't even enough room to hover properly. His wing tips nearly brushed the sides of the wretched walls every time he tried. There was just nothing to do in this stifling little room but go over it again and again in his mind.

He'd been floating near the top of the Oak that day, drifting in the breeze as it kissed the bright, feathery branches, making them sway back and forth like the wispy hair of an Angel. He'd been working on another song, for Fiona again, trying to get it right this time. His thoughts had been lost in lyrics and rhythms, trying to capture the essence of his best friend, as if that was a simple matter, when all of a sudden she'd been there, standing at the base of the Oak.

He wiped the sweat from his forehead and smiled, in spite of everything, at the thought of her. He hoped she wasn't up to something rash, though he was a little surprised there hadn't been any strange explosions yet.

His fingers brushed his temple and down his cheekbone, across the new tattoo of twisting ivy vines that was still healing. The sweat gathering in the tips of his dark hair sent stinging, salty beads running over the sensitive skin. He could hear his mother now, her voice echoing in his mind, reminding him that he was the one who felt it necessary to color his body with thistle ink. He laughed. She was right about that.

The truth was, she didn't really mind. Caelia didn't care what he did as long as he fulfilled his duties as Guardian. That was always their issue. He didn't want to be Guardian of the Rowan Oak, regardless of how honorable the post was, or how many of his family had done it before him. So his last name was Rowan. Did that mean he had to be the next Guardian? His mother thought so.

But he didn't want to spend his days flitting about the Oak waiting to protect it. No matter how grand the stories of the good old days were, no one cared about it anymore. It was a joke. No one really believed in its legendary power. The few creatures who might happen by did so for a good laugh, and that was all.

What he wanted was to make music, and explore the kingdom a bit. There was a whole world outside of the Enchanted Wood, or so Fiona always said. He meant to see some of it, hopefully with her and Manzy, before he faded into translucence. So when he'd seen her, unexpectedly standing at the bottom of the Oak that day, he was anxious to hear where she'd been.

She'd stood below, he remembered, not curled up on the ground like usual, or even leaning against her favorite spot where the bark had worn smooth. She'd had something in her hand, something she was looking at quite intently, and hadn't noticed him.

He'd flown behind the trunk of the Oak, floating down from the top so he could surprise her. Sneaking up on Fee was not an easy thing, and if he could manage this, he'd thought, he'd make sure she never heard the end of it.

"Gotcha!" he'd cried, popping out from behind the trunk.

"Hello, Jaydin," she'd said, looking up at him. She hadn't even flinched.

A goosechill ran over his body despite the sweltering warmth of his cell as he remembered the look she'd given him. It wasn't like her. He'd known Fiona Thorn for most of both their lives, since the time his mother had glittergilded his wing tips and drug him to the Dappled Forest for Fiona's Match Day ceremony. At three he'd had no interest in the little orphan that had been found along the banks of the Winding River the year before, or with the Bright Eye foal she'd be paired with. Now he counted them both as his closest friends.

Fiona could be rude, sarcastic, even nasty at times. But there'd been a darkness behind her eyes that day at the Oak that he'd never seen before. And never wished to see again.

He stood and glided softly around the room, his small circular path echoing the circles of his mind. So much had happened since then, to him and to the poor boy. But whenever he remembered that day, it always came back to her look. It was just off somehow, he felt it in his bones.

A noise outside the door drew his attention. He looked up in time to see one of the guards sliding a wooden tray of food through the door.

"Hey, Bo," Jaydin said, greeting the grufty old guard. His eyes flicked to the grayish lump on the tray. "What is it today? Any fruit this time?"

"'Fraid not, boy," Bo answered. "Looks like boiled boar's tongue again."

Jaydin smirked at the big man. Bo had been decent to him these last two turns, just a man doing his job.

"Could you ask again for me?"

"Sure kid. I'll ask."

Bo stepped out, pulling the door closed behind him. "Seems like an awful shame," he mumbled as he left.

Jaydin leaned his head against the old wooden door. "What's that?"

"You seem like a nice kid is all," Bo said. His voice was gruff as it came through the door. "Word is, they're gonna' hang ya', and soon. But I guess you'd know that, with your magic and all."

Jaydin's face paled to an ashy grey. They were really going to go through with it. "It doesn't work like that. My magic, I mean," he answered through the door. "I can hardly even fly in here."

"Sorry to hear that, I guess," Bo said. "I used to worry you'd fly out in the middle of the night and then they'd have me to blame."

Jaydin glanced at the tiny window on the other side of the room. It was so small he could barely see out. The idea of flying through it seemed funny. He laughed, the absurdity of his situation making him feel kind of crazy.

He rested his head on the door, listening as Bo's footsteps echoed all the way to the bottom. By his feet he saw the slimy chunk of boiled meat. Wonderful. He slid the tray with his foot and glided back to the far wall. He fanned his wings and slid back down.

His thoughts turned, as always, to that day at the Oak.

"Did I scare you?" he'd asked her, ignoring the chill behind her eyes.

"Not at all," she'd said, looking back at the gleaming thing in her hands.

"Where's Manzy?"

"Who?"

"Oh," he'd said, laughing, "it's like that? Whatever, Fee."

He'd flown from behind the tree and circled behind her, hovering above her shoulder to get a better look at what she'd had in her hands. It looked like a flute.

"Whatcha' got there?" he'd asked, noticing how the light danced on the silver instrument. He'd instantly hoped it was a present for him.

She balanced it on her palm, reaching to within inches of his face. "You mean this?"

She'd smiled and the wispy tip of a cobweb dangled from the corner of her mouth.

"Yes, Fiona! I mean that." He'd reached for it, but she'd snatched it away and hidden it behind her back. She danced behind the tree, laughing.

"Come on, Fee, let me see it."

"Okay," she'd said, peeking her head around the trunk. "But only if you'll play something."

He'd been incredulous. He'd stood in front of the Oak, hands on his hips. "*If* I'll play something? Seriously Fiona, have we met?" He'd motioned for her to hand it over, laughing at the game. "Give me the flute and I'll play whatever you want."

"Oh look," she'd said, pointing behind him, "you have company." She'd stuck her bottom lip out and ducked behind the trunk. "I guess it will have to wait."

He looked up at the gray stone ceiling as he remembered. He rubbed his sweaty face with his hands. How he'd wanted that flute! He'd never seen an instrument so perfect, not in all of his fifteen years.

He'd wanted to play it, immediately. And then, of course, his duties had gotten in the way. He'd turned to see what Fiona had been pointing at, and that's when he'd seen them. He could still see the boy as he'd been that day, bouncing up and down beside his travel worn father, eager as any light heart to see the Rowan Oak.

"Welcome!" Jaydin had called as they walked closer. Perhaps the sooner he showed them around, the sooner he could get back to that flute.

"Hi!" the boy had called, his bright smile stretching from ear to ear as he drug his father behind him. "We've come to see the Oak. Does it really tell your future? I want to be captain of a mighty ship one day! Can I see that? Can it tell my future?"

"Of course not, Brent," his father had said. "It's not real." He'd looked at Jaydin and scoffed. "Just fairy tricks and nonsense."

Jaydin had smiled at Brent, ignoring the father, and knelt in front of the boy. "Would you like to see what's possible, young man?"

"Yes please, Mr. Fairy, sir!"

"Call me Jaydin," he'd said, and winked at Brent. "Let's save 'sir' for the old bones, huh?"

Brent had laughed and reached for Jaydin's hand, then looked up at his father, making sure it was alright.

"Go on then, boy," Gantry mumbled. "I'll wait here."

Gantry had stood just outside the clearing that surrounded the Oak, rolling his watery eyes, wishing they'd get on with it so he could get his boy and his load of iron ore back to town.

"Jaydin?" Fiona had said, stepping from behind the tree, "maybe you could play for us." The deep blue and green spots of the feathered branches, like eyes of a peacock feather, reflected in the flute's shining surface.

"Would you like that?" he'd asked the boy.

"Yes please, Mr. Fairy, sir!"

Jaydin's eyes widened with mock irritation.

"I mean, yes please, Mr. Jaydin."

He'd ruffled Brent's blonde hair. "Just Jaydin, okay?"

Brent smiled sheepishly. "Okay."

Fiona handed Jaydin the flute, her face alive with excitement.

"What should I play?" he'd asked.

"Just look at the boy," she'd said. "Concentrate on him and I bet the magic will happen."

Brent had laughed and shrugged his shoulders, but Jaydin had smiled and did as she'd suggested, concentrating on the little boy as he put the flute to his lips. He'd been shocked by how warm it'd felt, nothing like the cool metal he'd been expecting. And when he began to play his first sensation was that the flute was pulsing, almost with a life of its own. It'd been disconcerting at first, frightening even, but as he'd continued to play, the music had carried his heart with its flowing rhythms, filling his mind with its soft, enchanting melody until there was nothing he could hear or see or think of but the music.

What had happened? he thought, resting his hands on his knees as he sat in the sweaty cell. *One minute I was playing the flute, and the next minute, everything was wrong.*

"Brent!!!"

The spell was broken as Gantry Neulock's voice had rumbled through the summer air. He'd rushed to his son, who lay crumpled on the ground, unmoving. The boy's eyes were open, but had glazed over, staring into nothingness.

Jaydin dropped the flute and felt the boy's forehead. It was ice cold.

"What happened?" he'd asked Gantry. "Is he sick?"

"As if you don't know," Gantry had spat at him.

"I don't...," Jaydin began, flustered by the man's accusation. "I don't know what happened at all! Please sir, let me help. I can take him to my mother," Jaydin had said, reaching to scoop Brent from the ground.

The man shoved Jaydin, sending him skittering backward. "Get your filthy hands off him!" he'd snarled. "What did you do? What sort of evil is this?"

"I don't know," Jaydin pleaded. "Honestly, I don't. Please. My mother can help him. She's not far."

Gantry gathered his son into his arms and glared at Jaydin. "You won't get away with this, fairy!"

And then he was gone, running from the Enchanted Wood.

He'd stood for a minute, watching them go. His mind couldn't make sense of it. How suddenly everything had changed.

"Fee, did you see that?" he'd asked, turning around.

But she and the flute had been gone.

He climbed to his feet and stood in the middle of the Tower room, his fingers laced behind his head. One minute she'd been there, with the most magical flute he'd ever seen, and the next, she was just gone. She'd vanished so quickly it was almost like she hadn't really been there at all.

9

Wilkes and Cal

For a second, time seemed to stand still. Fiona saw Graven's men coming at them, closing in on her and Rhiannon, but somehow they were moving slowly, like they were trudging through thick mud or impossibly deep snow.

And then everything sped up, and it all happened at once.

Rhiannon scrambled backward on her hands and feet, like a sparkly, skittering crab, and ran into Fiona, who was already up, digging in her satchel.

"THERE!" Fiona shouted, pointing to the desk, "with Isabel!"

Rhiannon crawled to her feet, narrowly escaping the mossy-toothed henchmen who was reaching for her leg. "AHHH!" she cried, frantically searching for some kind of weapon. She skidded into the desk and grabbed a few quills, hoping the pointed tips would be enough.

"DUCK!" Fiona shouted, and tossed her handful of Blast at the short man who was coming fast. At the same time, Cricket popped up from behind one of the leather chairs.

The little princess sent Kevin hurling toward the man, lashing the snake like a whip. Her chubby hands gripped his tail as he flew toward the target. Kevin's body stretched, his mouth open wide as he bared his long, sharp fangs.

"AAIIEEE!!!" he cried, shooting through the air. He hit dead on, sinking his teeth into the man's thigh. The man fell to his knees screaming, just before Fiona's explosive made contact.

Not exactly what I had in mind, Fiona thought from across the room, but it'll work.

The room exploded in a hail of dust and debris. The blast knocked Cricket to her bottom and shook Kevin from her grip. He slithered across the floor toward the door, with Cricket scrambling behind.

"AKE! AKE!"

The other one, the ugly tall man, was face down by the leather chairs, flattened by the explosion, but slowly began to stir. His eyes locked on Cricket. He snagged the hem of her skirt with two fingers and pulled her to the floor. He smiled, holding her down with one hand, and crawled to his feet.

"That's my princess, scumbag!" Fiona growled, stomping his hand with her boot. "But you can have this," she said, and elbowed him in the face. He grabbed his nose, blood spraying between his fingers, and fell backward, moaning. Fiona grabbed Cricket and ducked behind the desk.

"Thanks," Rhiannon said breathlessly as Fiona handed the little girl over.

"No problem," Fiona said, "she's my favorite."

The short man lay crumpled in the middle of the floor, shaking his head as he regained consciousness. He rubbed his thigh, cursing about being shot in the leg with some kind of arrow.

Behind the desk, Isabel was shaking, rocking back and forth. "This is bad. This is so bad."

"I have an idea," Rhiannon said. She peeked over the desk, still holding Cricket on her hip. The men were laying on the floor, arguing. The stocky one was holding his leg, trying to tear a hole in his pants.

"Well?" Fiona asked. "We don't have much time."

Rhiannon crouched back down. "We can go through the tunnels."

Isabel's eyes widened. "No, Rhi!"

"I don't think we have much choice."

Isabel wrapped her arms around herself and began to whimper.

Fiona looked at the two of them. Unbelievable. They could even bicker at a time like this. "The what?" she asked.

"The tunnels." Rhiannon said, ignoring Isabel. "The only thing is, it's over there." She pointed toward the other side of the room.

"That looks like a closet," Fiona said.

"It IS a closet," Isabel cried angrily through her tears, "only there's a door in the back that goes to the tunnels."

"Excuse me," Fiona snapped, "for not being familiar with the secret passage in the King's chambers." Exactly why she worked alone. Partnerships were overrated, especially whiny, frilly ones.

"She's afraid of the tunnels," Rhiannon said. "It's dark and wet."

"But how will we even get there? They'll get us!" Isabel said, wiping her tears with the back of her hand.

"I'll distract them," Fiona said, patting her bag. "Okay," she continued, "I'm going to toss a Smoker out there. Then we run for it. Got it?"

Cricket laughed and shouted, "Got it!"

"On three," Fiona whispered, reaching into her bag. Her fingers deftly rifled through her supplies. When they landed on the right squishy wad, she ripped a hunk off and held it up. "One, two," she stood and quickly tossed a black ball into the room. "Three!"

As soon as the ball hit the floor it erupted in a plume of thick, gray smoke. Within seconds its dark fog had spread, filling the entire room. The smoke settled in a heavy haze that floated just above the floor.

Fiona grabbed Rhiannon's arm. "Stay down. Crawl for the closet!"

Rhiannon nodded and led the way. Cricket followed, with Isabel and Fiona bringing up the rear.

A muffled quiet had settled in the smoky room. The men weren't arguing anymore. They're out there though, Fiona thought, listening for us to make a sound. Listening for us to make a mistake. The girls crawled quickly, passing the two leather chairs with no sign of either men.

Fiona could see through a slight clearing on the bottom of the haze that they were almost to the closet. Just a few more feet and Rhiannon would make it. She felt like her feet were dangling in an ocean swimming with sharks. The two of them were out there, somewhere. She could feel them, just waiting to attack.

Rhiannon opened the closet and was climbing through when something fell over, crashing loudly to their left. Fiona's heart thumped in her throat, pounding so hard she could barely breath. She watched the others crawl in, one by one. Isabel was almost through. Just one more second and she could go.

Something grabbed Fiona from behind. A thick, heavy hand wrapped its fingers around her right ankle and began pulling. She had nothing to grip with her hands, nothing to fight the force of being pulled backward.

The fingers tightened and pulled, harder. She felt the cool stone sliding across her stomach as she slid backward.

"GET OFF!" she shouted, and kicked as hard as she could, the frustration of the whole day blasting out through her foot. The heavy treads of her boot connected with something round and slippery, she heard a very satisfying CRUNCH! followed by a man swearing, and then she was free. She flew into the closet, knocking everyone else over.

The girls scrambled to their feet. They pushed through the hanging cloaks and robes and ducked through the small opening in the back of the closet.

"What now?" Fiona asked, coughing. She looked at Rhiannon. Hopefully there was more to this plan than crawling through the back of a closet. Though, she grudgingly admitted, it had worked. So far.

They stood in a dark hallway made of stone. The ceiling arched above them and while they had plenty of room to stand up, the passage was not very wide. They moved forward slowly, single file, adjusting to their new surroundings as they fought to catch their breath.

"I don't think they'll follow us," Rhiannon said, laughing nervously. "They're probably standing in front of the closet right now, wondering what happened. They didn't seem very smart."

"So what are we going to do?" Isabel asked.

"We follow this for awhile. There's a door up ahead that will take us to the kitchen. I do it all the time."

The stone was damp and the darkness echoed with their footsteps. Small torches were hung sparsely along the wall, the flickering light casting ghostly shadows as they moved. It smelled dirty and musty, and vaguely of animal, like an old dog who'd just come in from the rain. Only not as friendly.

"Good. I'm starving," Fiona said, relaxing a bit. They might get through this yet.

"Me too," said a squeaky, high-pitched voice from behind her.

Fiona's blood ran cold. Her stomach lurched and she swung around, knowing what she would find.

The tall ugly one was there, his face plastered with a stupid grin. He was too tall to stand up, so he hovered, looking down at her with his head tilted at a weird angle. His arms reached out, stretching from one wall of the tunnel to the other.

"How 'bout you, Wilkes?" he said through his grotesque smile, this time in his normal voice.

The stocky one poked his head from behind his partner and smiled menacingly at the cluster of frightened girls. "Yeah, Cal. I always have room for a snack." He ran his tongue over his chapped lips and nodded. The stink of his breath moved through the stale air, reaching Fiona's face.

"RUN!!!!" she cried.

Rhiannon grabbed Cricket and the girls took off. Behind them the two men sprang into action as well. The short one in back, Wilkes, shoved his partner from behind and ended up knocking him over. Cal tripped and fell, his long legs and arms flinging in all directions as he went down, making him look like a giraffe on ice skates. Wilkes climbed over him and accidentally stepped on his throat.

"OW!" Cal squeeked.

"Get up, will ya'?" Wilkes called, looking over his shoulder as he stumbled ahead. "Come on!"

Rhiannon led them further under the castle, following her familiar path to the secret kitchen door. "Come on!" she said as they rounded a corner. "It's just ahead."

They wasted no time, knowing the men couldn't be far behind. Their voices bounced off the stone walls, surrounding the girls as they ran.

"Here. This one," Rhiannon said, catching her breath. She put Cricket down and reached for the door. She turned the handle, but nothing happened. She twisted harder, furiously shaking it back and forth.

"It's locked!" she cried, looking over her shoulder at the other girls. She pounded on the door with her fists.

"HELP!" Rhiannon cried to anyone who might be listening on the other side.

"That's great," Fiona said, kneeling as she gasped for breath. Who's going to be standing in the back of a huge kitchen pantry, she thought, on the other side of a secret door?

"Come out, come out, wherever you are!" Wilkes' voice echoed around them, getting louder with each second.

"This isn't working!" Fiona hissed. "Keep going! Go! Run!"

Rhiannon looked at her, defeated. "I don't know any other way out!"

"Just run!" Fiona shouted.

They ran hard, trying to make up for lost time. Every time they thought they were spreading the gap, Wilkes' voice would find them, his threats floating forward in the damp air.

There was no pattern to discover, nothing to help them figure out where they were or where they were going. The flickering shadows stretched long on the stone walls as the torches got farther apart and the darkness of the tunnels grew heavy. Fiona tried each door they found, but they were all locked.

The dark path twisted back and forth with no reason or sense. The only thing they knew for certain was that they were headed down. The angle of the floor had become increasingly steep, sending them farther below the ground and farther away from the castle with every step.

"Come on, girls!" Wilkes called. "We just want to talk to ya'! That's all." The gravelly voice reached out from behind, closing in.

"That's not true, is it Wilkes?" Cal whispered to his partner, a bit too loud. "I thought sure we was gonna' have to drag 'em back to the boss."

"Shut up, will ya'?"

The girls skidded to a stop. The tunnel had dumped them into a circular room. A large wooden door hung open to the left, and in front was a staircase. To their right they saw nothing but more thick, stone wall.

"In here!" Fiona whispered, hustling everyone through the open door.

The girls ran through and quietly closed the door, huddling on the other side.

"Rhi, what are we doing?" Isabel asked, her tear streaked face looking up at her sister.

"Sshh!" Fiona snapped, fighting to catch her breath. "We'll wait here until they run by, up the stairs. Then we can sneak out and go back the way we came."

Isabel nodded and smiled at Fiona.

They huddled together, waiting anxiously for the men to pass. The footsteps grew louder, coming closer down the tunnel, until the sound of the men's panting breath filled the chamber and Fiona knew they were just outside the door.

"What's this then?" Cal croaked. "Up the steps?"

"Well," Wilkes said, drawing out his words, "if you was a pretty princess, which way would you go?"

"I'd go up the steps."

"Really?" Wilkes answered, stepping closer to the door. "Not me. I'd go through this door right here," and he pounded his fist into the door twice.

BANG! BANG!

The girls jumped. Rhiannon's eyes widened and she looked at Fiona. Fiona raised a finger to her lips, pleading with the princesses to keep it together.

"But all these doors is locked, Wilkes," Cal said, sitting on the stone floor.

"Oh, not this one." He turned to Cal. "I left it open last night. My hands was full, and I didn't bother closin' it."

~ 50 ~

Fiona's head slumped on her shoulders and she shook her head. She hadn't seen that coming.

Isabel saw Fiona's reaction and started crying again. Which made Cricket growl.

Cal jumped to his feet and looked around the chamber. "What's that? What's that noise?"

"That's nothin', Cal," Wilkes said. Fiona could almost feel his creepy smile crawling up her spine through the door. "That's just the sound pretty little rats make when they're trapped."

Cal's smile spread slowly across his ugly face.

Wilkes reached for his belt and removed a large set of keys. They clinked loudly in the chamber, jostling and clanging as he sifted through them, until finally he selected the right one. He reached out and locked the door.

"Guess that takes care of that!" Wilkes said, turning to Cal. The sound of his laughter mingled with the jingling keys as he secured them to his belt.

Wilkes turned to go, gesturing for Cal to lead the way.

"But hang on," Cal said, his hand scratching his head, "isn't we supposed to bring them back to the boss?"

"Think Cal!" Wilkes spat, tapping his head with a thick, sausage finger as he outlined the genius of his plan. "We do this, it saves the boss a step. He'll thank us."

"I dunno," Cal said, shaking his head. "Them's princesses in there," he whispered, urging Wilkes to see reason. "Lockin' that door's as good as killin' the King's own daughters. There's no way out of there! Nothing down there but old storage tunnels. They'll starve!"

"That's right!" Rhiannon shouted, pounding from the other side of the door. "We ARE princesses and my father will never allow this! Let us out this instant!"

Both men turned to the door, the princesses' cries now mingling with the steady protective growling coming from the other side. Cal pleaded with his partner to stick to the plan.

But Wilkes was ambitious. He prided himself on being a man who knew opportunity when it came knocking, or pounding.

"Just hang on, now! All of ya'," he shouted. He leaned his head against the door. "You won't starve, pretty princesses. Not right away. Last time I was down there I saw plenty of rats." He looked at Cal and laughed.

"I dunno, Wilkes," Cal said, shaking his head, "it still don't seem right. Leavin' those girls like that."

"I'll tell you what ain't right!" Wilkes shouted, cramming his finger in Cal's face. "Servin' a King who loves them mixed breeds and flittin' fairys so much! But we won't for long if Graven has his way. Now come on," he said, stomping up the stairs, "we'd be taking care of it one way or another. Now it's done."

"But Wilkes, them's just kids in there!"

Wilkes jumped down and grabbed Cal by the front of his shirt. And despite their difference in size, he slammed the tall man against the stone wall.

"How would you like to join them on the other side of that door? Huh?" Cal hung limp in the stout man's hands like an old rag doll, his watery eyes looking away from Wilkes. "Now keep your mouth shut and let's go."

Rhiannon shouted and pounded on the door long after the men's footsteps had dwindled away, leaving nothing but empty silence on the other side. But it was no use. Wilkes had gotten his way. They were alone, buried deep within the dark, wandering tunnels that stretched under the castle, with nothing to eat.

Well, nothing besides the rats.

10

A Fine Mess

Stars dotted the night sky. Their white light glinted on his body as it slid swiftly over the hard ground, flying down the cart path that led back to the barn. His jet black scales all but disappeared under the deepening cover of darkness. Luckily there weren't any people on the path to be avoided at this hour. He had no time to play hide and seek with villagers tonight. Yes, luckily it was night time.

Except that was where their luck had run out.

By Heaven's Gate this was a fine mess, with the potential to go all wrong if he didn't get a handle on things. Her Eminence would not be pleased if months of work from multiple agents came to nothing. At least he hadn't been compromised. No one had seen him.

It was all so much worse than any of his classified information had led him to believe. Even worse than the time he'd been stuck for more than a year in deep cover, caught in the middle of that never-ending dispute between the Giants of Donner.

He took a deep breath and allowed the fresh air to penetrate the full length of his body. It refreshed his tense, jittery muscles.

So it was Graven. Raptor had been right about that. But the old man seemed anxious, all of a sudden, making snap decisions and moving faster than they'd expected. Bright Eye sources had watched him patiently maneuvering in the shadows for so long, and now, this? They'd suspected he was after the King, and certainly the fairy, he'd made no secret of that. But to order the princesses held and brought to him by those thugs? It was beyond reckless. It was desperate.

Desperate and reckless, Kevin thought. *That equaled dangerous. Very dangerous.*

Things had gotten out of hand. One minute he was pleasantly coiled around Cricket and the next he was flying through the air in a lightning strike, baring his fangs at hostiles. The corner of his wide mouth lifted in a smile. By the Angels that one was a fierce little fighter! And her aim was legitimate.

At least he'd managed to keep those mercenaries busy long enough for the girls to get away. Fiona's Smoker had been the perfect diversion. While Graven's minions were stumbling around above, choking on the bad air and knocking into everything, he'd been sliding around below. He'd gotten under their feet and tripped them up more times than he could count.

When he'd seen the girls heading for the closet, he figured they'd formed an evacuation plan. He had to believe that. Though he hadn't expected them to know about the King's secret escape route into the tunnels. That was impressive. Not many did.

He shook his head and smiled again. He would have to stop underestimating these girls.

But what if they were followed after you left?

His mind twisted in every direction, leaving him no peace. They were never supposed to be involved in this! This was not the plan.

He took another deep breath and tried to remember his training.

Missions are fluid. Plans evolve. Don't get involved.

A bit late on that last one though, and he knew it. He was undeniably involved now, responsible even, and that made it different. Harder. Everything that it wasn't supposed to be. It made it personal.

His eyes closed to menacing slits and flashed with anger. If anything happened to those girls...especially Cricket.

His anger cooled, fading into the familiar anxiety he felt when he was on a mission. Adrenaline pulsed through his system, urging him forward as he caught sight of the barn. *Almost there now.* He sped up, anxious to find Manzy.

He slithered from the path into the grass by the barn, where they had left her a few hours before, grazing on fresh dandelion greens.

A few hours ago. When everything still made sense. When the hard target had been the King, not his daughters. What was Graven doing?

But she wasn't here. Where could she be? She knew the plan. She knew they were supposed to meet back here.

He slid silently into the dark barn, over the hard-packed dirt floor, looking everywhere for Manzy. Prince and Midnight stood contentedly grazing in their stalls to the left. They hadn't even noticed his presence. Good thing, too, he thought. Nothing sent a horse over the edge faster than a snake on the ground. He smiled sheepishly to himself. He still owed Isabel an apology for this afternoon on the Plains. But hey, a guy had to eat.

His thoughts were all over as he flew back out of the barn, sliding through the dust like a living whip.

He had to find Manzy. She knew Fiona better than anyone, and chances were good that the princesses would follow the girl's lead. But where would she take them?

He took another breath and reminded himself they'd gone into the tunnels, clearly on purpose. He'd seen them, he'd even helped make sure they made it. They must have had a reason, a way out.

If only he could find Manzy. Together they could form a new plan. One that included finding the girls, or saving them. He just didn't know. There was so little information! Mix that with the distressing fact that he cared about those girls and you had a spy's worst nightmare.

He turned left, and headed behind the barn. Huge piles of manure stood, waiting to be spread in the surrounding fields. The weeds were much taller here, too. He couldn't see a thing.

"Manzy," he whispered. "Manzy? Manzanita Rose?"

Something moved behind one of the piles. A white head lifted and looked around.

"Manzy!" he said, breathing a huge sigh of relief. "Down here."

She stepped from behind the pile of manure and walked toward the sound of his voice.

"There you are," she said, looking down at where he was coiled in the weeds. "I thought you were never coming back."

She reached around with her head and itched a troublesome spot on her left flank. Her back left foot raised slightly, pawing gently in the air as she carefully nibbled her hide. "Did you get what you came for?" she asked after dealing with the bothersome itch.

"Manzy," Kevin began, "we've got a problem."

"What do you mean? What happened?"

She stood at full alert, sensing the concern in her old friend's voice. She stretched her neck down to the ground and pricked her ears toward Kevin.

"It's Graven."

"Oh," she breathed, blowing heavily through her nostrils, "I see. Well, I can't say that I'm surprised. I thought something had happened to the girls. By Heaven's Gate, Kevin! Don't scare me like that."

She raised her head and shook it back and forth, releasing some of the tension. Her long mane nearly glowed as it twisted through the night air, then came to rest, gently cascading down her neck.

"It is about the girls, Manzy."

Kevin looked at her from under his thick eyelashes, the worry in his dark eyes all too plain. She stiffened and lowered her head once more.

"Tell me everything."

11

Winkle

"HELP! HELP US! PLEASE! SOMEONE!"

Fiona sat on the ground, her back against the stone wall, listening to Rhiannon and Isabel shout for help. Cricket was with them, screaming something guttural and incoherent as she kicked the door.

Fiona rubbed her hands down the front of her dirty pants and exhaled. She was still tired from running and was having trouble getting enough air.

"I don't think anyone can hear you," she said between breaths, watching them pound on the door. "You've been at it for over an hour. You might as well save your strength." She looked down and scanned the darkness of the room. "I have a feeling you're going to need it."

Their prison was a large room with a short hallway to the left. It led to another, smaller room. Both were bare, except for a bunch of old wooden crates and some glass bottles in the smaller room. The walls were cold stone, and probably the ceiling too, though it was too high for any of them to be sure. The floor was also cold, but it was hard-packed dirt. And it was dark. Very dark.

"Well we have to do something," Rhiannon said. "Graven is after my father! You heard him! I don't know what that old man thinks he's going to do, but I have to stop him! And in case you haven't noticed, we're locked in some stupid storage room below the castle!"

She paced back and forth like an angry peacock, then stopped in front of Fiona. "We can't just sit here and do nothing!"

The yellowish light coming from the small hunk of Glow Fiona had activated was beginning to dim. Its faint burn flickered briefly, casting an eerie haze onto all of their faces.

"I agree," Fiona said, "but this screaming thing you're doing just isn't working!" She climbed to her feet, angry all of a sudden, and stood in front of Rhiannon. "And it's beginning to get on my NERVES!"

Cricket looked at Fiona and began a low, rumbling growl.

"Listen you vicious little jelly bean," Fiona said, glaring at the girl, "I'm not really in the mood. I've got bigger problems than you right now."

"Leave her out of it. If it wasn't for your brilliant idea we wouldn't even be here!" Rhiannon shouted.

"Let's go in the tunnels," Fiona chimed in a snotty princess voice. "I can get us out through a door into the *KITCHEN!* Ring any bells? Yeah, all my idea."

"Stop it! Both of you!" Isabel yelled. "What are we going to do? I can't eat rats. I don't even want to SEE any rats." She began sobbing again.

Cricket plopped down on the floor beside Rhiannon and looked up expectantly, waiting for instructions.

"I don't know what we're going to do yet, Izzy," Rhiannon said, rubbing the top of Cricket's head. "But nobody is eating any rats." Then she turned back to Fiona and mumbled, "And I didn't know the stupid door would be locked."

"Well I didn't know they would lock this stupid door!" Fiona fumed, irritated that she'd been so careless. "And anyone who isn't a spoiled little princess would know that rat isn't that bad. So there."

They looked at each other for a minute, then both started laughing.

"You've eaten a rat?" Rhiannon asked, scrunching her face.

Fiona shrugged her shoulders. "And mudslickers, too. Rats are way better."

"I don't wanna eat rats!" Isabel moaned.

"You will if you get hungry enough," Fiona said. *And that'll be sooner than you think.* She'd finished the last roll of her plum leather that morning, when she and Manzy had stopped by the river. There wasn't so much as a crumb of barley cake in her pack. She'd already checked.

Cricket began bouncing around Rhiannon's legs, pulling on her skirts. "Ake, Rhi? Ake?"

"What?"

"She's looking for Kevin," Isabel mumbled. "She misses him. And so do I." She started crying again.

"Give it a rest, Izzy," Rhiannon said. "I can't think with you whining all the time!"

Isabel slid down the wall and hunched in a ball, sobbing to herself.

Rhiannon shook her head and looked at Cricket. She was still pulling on her skirts and calling for her missing serpent.

"Not right now, Cricket. Sorry."

Cricket hung her head, her wispy blond hair dangling in her eyes, and slowly walked away, wandering through the darkness calling, "AKE! AKE!"

"AHHHH!"

"What? Izzy, what is it?"

"Something just ran by my foot! I could feel it!" She put her hands over her face and screamed. "It had a big, long tail. It touched my foot!!"

"Isabel, honestly!" Rhiannon said. "It's probably just a mouse. Unless all those cuts on your arms are drawing the rats out." She smiled wickedly in the dark. "Maybe they can smell your blood."

"AHHHH! Get them away from my blood!"

"Enough," Fiona said, leaving no doubt in any of their royal little heads who was running the show.

Fiona crouched in front of Isabel. "Calm down. Stop screaming."

She reached in her pack and pulled out a large wooden stick. "Here. If you feel anything, whack it with this. Just make sure it isn't one of us."

Isabel hesitated, then took the thick, bark-covered club. "But, won't it hurt me when it blows up? I mean, how do I make it work? What is it anyway?"

"It's a stick."

Isabel smiled a little through her tears. "Oh."

"If you don't hurt yourself with it," Fiona said, smiling, "maybe tomorrow I'll find you something that goes bang."

"Okay." Isabel leaned against the wall and gripped her stick tightly, feeling a little better now that she was armed.

"So, any ideas?" Rhiannon asked as Fiona walked back toward her. "Can you blow us out of here or something?"

"I do have more Blast, but it would probably kill us when the roof caved in. Escape routes are less effective when you've been crushed to death." She laughed and patted her head. "Before Lighting Always Secure the Top."

"Huh?"

"Nothing. Just something McClane says. Anyway, it's not my first choice."

"Who's McClane?"

"No one," Fiona said, closing the door to her other life. The life without whining princesses and rats. "Nevermind."

"What about Manzy?"

"What about her?"

"Send her a message or something and tell her we need help," Rhiannon said confidently.

Fiona smirked. Every time she thought the girl might have something going on upstairs, she went and said something like that. Clearly she had no idea how desperate their situation was.

"It doesn't work like that. We don't share a telepathic link." She shook her head. "I talk to her just like I'm talking to you. She can't hear me from down here." She looked Rhiannon in the eye. "We're on our own."

Rhiannon smiled wistfully. "It's still pretty cool. The way you can talk to her, I mean." She rustled her skirts and leaned against the wall. "What will she think when you don't come back? What will she do?"

"She'll go to our meeting place." Fiona looked at Rhiannon, measuring her with a hard gaze. "Getting out of here is our concern," she said, feeling the familiar shortness of breath and tickle in the back of her throat. "We do that, and I'll get us to Manzy."

"And then we help my father?"

"And then we help Jaydin," she said as the coughing overtook her. She leaned against the wall until it was over. "And your father," she said as she stood, rubbing her face in her hands.

Rhiannon and Fiona worked most of that night, spending hours exploring the dark edges of their dungeon. They took turns with the small bit of Glow, each one holding it in front as they searched the textured bumps and cracks of the rough walls. They searched the hallway and the small room.

For awhile, Cricket stayed with them. She wandered the large room by herself, still looking for Kevin. When she toddled back to Rhiannon late in the night, swinging a very large, dead rat by its tail, both older girls agreed it was an especially good thing that Isabel had cried herself to sleep long ago.

For hours they found nothing. Then, during a short break, Fiona stretched her arms above her head, trying to ease the cramps in her back and shoulders. Even in the faint light from the dying wad of Glow that she held in one hand it was obvious what they were. Fiona reached for Rhiannon, tugging at her arm.

"Look up."

Dangling from the dark ceiling of the large room, everywhere they looked, were bunches of Shadowbells. The drying flowers hung overhead like a death sentence.

"That's why Wilkes was down here," Fiona whispered, the truth becoming all too clear. "That's why this door was open." She looked at Rhiannon, wondering if she was connecting the dots also.

"Graven," she hissed. "He's going to poison my father. Not just the fairy, but Father too. He's planning on killing them both. With those."

Rhiannon gestured to the ceiling as she stomped around in the failing light, mumbling and cursing to herself. She bent over and started digging around on the ground for something. When she stood up, she held a big rock in her hand.

She looked up at the ceiling, aimed and pulled her arm back. But Fiona caught her by the elbow before she could throw the stone.

"What are you doing?"

"Let me go!" Rhiannon shouted, pulling free. "I'm gonna' smash his stupid poison flowers into a million pieces."

"You do that and we all die."

Rhiannon looked at her, not understanding.

"If you crush those dried petals, they'll poison the air we're stuck breathing. Got it?"

"We have to get out of here," Rhiannon said, slumping her shoulders. "I HAVE to get to my father." The rock fell to the dirt floor with a dull thud.

"And I have to get to Jaydin."

When the dim yellow light flickered and finally blinked out, leaving them in a darkness so black they couldn't see an inch in front of their faces, they kept going anyway. They saved the rest of the Glow, thinking they might need it for tomorrow. And silently hoped they wouldn't need it the day after that.

They walked the perimeter over and over, their hands cracked and bleeding from hours of running along the hard stone, quietly searching the same cold walls for any small hint of escape.

Eventually they gave in to their exhaustion and joined Isabel against the wall. They huddled together for warmth and settled in for a long night.

But Fiona couldn't sleep. Her thoughts were consumed by the debt she owed.

It'd been an easy decision. Reckless, no doubt, but easy. Despite Jaydin's innocence, the King seemed anxious to make an example of him, and word was quickly spreading that the fairy would hang. Even Caelia was at a loss.

So she'd gone to the Moonshadow.

She'd knelt on the mossy bank and asked to see what would save his life. For her trouble she'd gotten a vision of some creepy old woman covered in ice. And of course, the debt. For she'd had no way to make payment.

Look to know what you will, but pay in kind or winds will still.

She'd tossed a few bunches of willow root to the water, and some Demon's Tongue she'd found in her bag, just for good measure, and hoped it would be enough.

Apparently it was not. What did *pay in kind* mean anyway?

It didn't matter. Jaydin was the only friend she'd ever really had, next to Manzy, and her life wouldn't be worth much without him.

Yes, she thought, it'd been a very easy decision. The only thing that mattered now was getting him out of prison. And quickly too. She was sicker than she'd expected. Things were moving fast. She crossed her fingers and said a prayer to the Angels that she still had enough time.

She thought of the girls and the irritation of being stuck with them, and grudgingly realized she was developing a slow building respect for Rhiannon and the work she'd done that night. Sometimes people surprised you. Even frilly ones.

She thought of strategy and escape plans, of things she might be missing. But in the end she thought of Jaydin. She saw him in her mind, his bright green wings open behind him, the soft sun of the Wood glinting in his deep, brown eyes.

I wonder what he does in his stone cell, she thought as her eyes finally became heavy. She wrapped her arms around her pack and snuggled down, trying to still her shivering. She smiled at the irony, despite her weakening condition. Some rescue this was turning out to be.

****

"Wake up! Wake up!" Isabel stood over Rhiannon, shaking her shoulder. "Come on, GET UP!"

"WHAT?" Rhiannon yelled. She sat up, disoriented. She couldn't see anything in this blackness, not even her sister standing right over her. "What is it, Izzy? What's wrong?"

"It's Cricket," she said, feeling around the ground for Fiona's pack. "I can't find her."

"It's not like she can go anywhere," Fiona grumbled without opening her eyes. "And stay OUT of my pack." She grabbed her canvas bag and rolled over on her side so she was facing the wall. She'd had a restless night. Her chest was sore from coughing and she couldn't seem to get warm. She had a feeling she had a fever.

"Well, I need some Shine or Bright or whatever. I can't see anything. I need some light. Please."

"Isabel," Rhiannon said, slouching back against the wall, "Fiona's right. She can't go anywhere. She's fine."

"Come on you guys!" Isabel pleaded, "what about the rats?"

Rhiannon kicked Fiona lightly.

"Yeah, Fiona," Rhiannon said, remembering the special present her baby sister had brought them late last night, "we have to protect Cricket from the rats."

Fiona sat up, her weak grin concealed by the darkness. After they'd managed, with some effort, to get the dead rodent away from Cricket, she'd tucked it away in the farthest corner of the small room, hoping Isabel never had to see it. Or that she never had to hear Isabel after she saw it.

"More like the other way around," Fiona mumbled as she fumbled in her pack. She rolled two squishy wads back and forth in her palms until they began to glow with bright yellow light.

"Here," she said, handing one of the balls of Glow to Isabel. "Go look for her if you want."

"Aren't you guys coming?" she asked, taking the glowing ball.

"No," both older girls said at the same time.

"You guys are mean."

Isabel grabbed the stick that Fiona had given her the night before and walked off in search of her little sister. Her shouts for Cricket faded as she turned down the short hallway and headed for the smaller room.

"You look awful," Rhiannon said as the muted light washed over Fiona's face.

Fantastic, Fiona thought. Not only am I imprisoned in a dark cave, doomed to slowly sicken and die, but I have to hear how awful I look from Fancy Pants?

Fiona glared at Rhiannon and shook her head. "Haven't we been over this?"

"Sorry! You just look...I'm just worried."

"Well don't be. I'm fine," Fiona said. By Heaven's Gate, she thought, if there was any justice in the world being trapped with this one would be payment of a thousand debts.

"So what's the plan?"

"Keep looking for a way out, I guess," Fiona answered, shivering through a yawn.

"But we looked for hours last night and it's all the same," Rhiannon said, painfully close to a whine. Her stomach growled loudly. "We didn't find anything except for those stupid crates. There's no way out, other than the door."

"There's always a way. We just have to find it." Fiona crawled to her feet and held a hand out to Rhiannon. "Let's get to work."

****

Just a short distance away, Isabel was doing some work of her own. It was the first time she'd been exploring and so the sight of the wooden crates in the small room filled her with excitement.

She walked toward the far wall where a few of them stood stacked on top of one another and held the glowing light in front of her, looking closely.

Beside the fallen stack of crates was an opening.

It wasn't large, but it was easily big enough for her to crawl through. Her heart pounded with excitement.

She crouched in front of the opening, gathered her skirt in her hands and took a deep breath. Then, holding the ball of Glow in front of her, she crawled in.

The tunnel was damp, and smaller than she expected. Her hands felt muddy and gritty as she crawled through the tight space. She was almost to the other side when her knee bumped something.

"Eeee!" she screamed, shivering all over.

When it didn't move or try to bite her, she reached down with her hand. Bendy with long, stringy things. Definitely not a rat.

But her face fell as she raised it into the sphere of Glow.

Cricket's shoe.

"Cricket!"

She rushed through the rest of the tunnel and crawled out the opening, frantically searching for her little sister. Water seeped from the stone walls, making them glossy in the dim light, and the ceiling dripped. The air was heavy with the smell of salt water and it was very quiet except for the soft, slow trickle of dripping water. There was light coming from the other side of the room, through another, larger tunnel.

In the middle of the room, sitting on the muddy floor, was something Isabel had never seen before.

The creature was small with thin little arms and legs. It had a round body, and was covered in greenish-blue scales that glistened in the low light. Its full stomach rested on the ground between its two legs, which were splayed out in a V shape. On top of its tiny neck was a head so large it seemed too big for the rest of its body. And set deep in its big head was a pair of bulging round eyes that glowed the most vibrant shade of lavender she'd ever seen. They made Isabel think of a strange and wonderful fish.

Sitting beside the creature, holding its hand, was Cricket.

"Cricket! Are you okay?" Isabel cried, running forward with the shoe.

"Izzy!" Cricket called, climbing to her feet. Her short, wispy hair bounced in her eyes. She grabbed her shoe and put Isabel's hand in the outstretched hand of the creature.

The creature tilted her large head, following the activity with her big eyes.

Isabel watched as Cricket slipped her shoe on, giggled, then ran across the room and crawled back through the tunnel.

"Cricket wait!"

But she was already gone.

Isabel looked back and found the creature's huge eyes staring at her. The greenish-blue scales were warm in her hand.

She smiled and sat down.

It was mesmerizing. The big eyes were so round and bright, prettier than any of the bolts of luxurious fabric Miss Delia, the dress maker, had ever shown them. By far.

And it meant no harm, Isabel thought, anyone could see that. She wasn't afraid of it, exactly. But what was it?

There was definitely something girly about it, too, Isabel decided. So, it was a girl. *She* was a girl.

Isabel reached out and gripped the other scaly hand, surprised again at how warm it felt.

The creature smiled, making the tiny, colorful scales on her face shift. Isabel smiled back, and something in her shifted as well. She had made a new friend.

"You're very pretty," Izzy said, holding their hands up, "in a fishy kind of way."

The creature's eyes widened as she listened.

"I'm Izzy. What's your name?"

Its head tipped to the side, looking questioningly at Isabel.

"Can't you talk? Hmm, that's okay I guess. I can talk for both of us." She winked at the creature, swinging their hands back and forth gently between them.

The creature smiled and winked back.

"Hey! That was pretty good!"

The creature's smile widened and she winked a few more times, her bulging eyes flashing in the dim cave.

"Okay, okay, so you can wink," Isabel laughed. "Don't hurt yourself, Winky Winkleton." Isabel's eyes lit up. "That's it! I'll call you Winkle. How about that?"

Winkle smiled again, pleased with her new name.

"I'm a princess. Not that you can tell by any of this," Isabel said, looking down at her dress. Winkle hesitantly touched the dirty fabric of the dress.

Isabel watched as Winkle explored the texture of the fabric with her scaly fingers. As she held the cloth in her hand, the color of her eyes changed from bright violet to a soft yellow, then green, then back to the purple.

"WOOAH! You should see your eyes! That was cool!"

Winkle lifted her hands so they were resting beside her eyes. She smiled and her eyes glowed with every color of the rainbow, slowly fading from one color to the next, then flashing faster through the spectrum.

"AWESOME! Do it again!!"

Winkle shook her head and laughed, a small wet sound that reminded Isabel of the way Cricket used to burp when she was really little.

"Okay, I get it. I bet it makes you dizzy, huh?"

Winkle nodded and crawled to her feet.

For awhile they wandered the room together. Winkle showed Isabel where she slept, a sloppy little puddle that looked very unappealing to the princess. And Winkle listened as the princess asked every question that popped into her buzzing head. Isabel was just about to ask Winkle what she ate when the other girls stepped through the tunnel.

"Isabel!" Rhiannon called as she and Fiona rushed forward, "Be careful!"

Winkle's eyes flashed to a deep and threatening crimson. They burned in the low light like dangerous flames. Her breath became tight and fast; a wheezing sound that was frightening to hear.

"Relax," Fiona said, grabbing Rhiannon by the shoulder, "it's just a Cave Bodkin. They're usually pretty friendly."

"Don't, Rhi!" Isabel said, "You're scaring her!"

Isabel bent down and looked into Winkle's bright red eyes. "It's just my sister. She's like that sometimes."

Fiona smiled, delighted at their luck. Cave Bodkins were notorious for snaking their way through tight places.

"What is that, Izzy?" Rhiannon asked. She grimaced, giving Winkle the once over.

"I told you," Fiona said, "she's a Cave Bodkin. They're common in dark, damp areas, especially underground. And," she said, pointing to Winkle, "they're usually very social. Unless of course something frilly runs at them shouting." She shook her head.

Isabel held Winkle's hand, watching as her eyes faded from an angry red to burnt orange, calming yellow to soothing green, and through a dozen shades of blue before finally settling back to the vibrant lavender she loved so much.

"Rhi," she said, taking a deep breath, "don't be rude. Try again."

Isabel was about to introduce the girls when Winkle looked up at Rhiannon and started winking.

Isabel laughed. "Rhi, this is Winkle. She's my friend."

Rhiannon winced at the thought of touching the scaly little creature, but politely shook Winkle's hand.

Cricket bounced around beside Isabel. Winkle smiled, put a gentle hand on the little girl's head and winked a few more times.

"Wonder where the name came from," Fiona said, shaking her head.

"You two sure can pick 'em," Rhiannon said, watching her sisters.

"I don't suppose Winkle happens to know a way out of here," Fiona asked, knowing full well that any Cave Bodkin worth its salt knew three different ways out of a sewn up grain sack.

Isabel's face lit up like the rising dawn. Her eyes sparkled with triumph and pride. "As a matter of fact, she does."

****

In no time Winkle had the girls running swiftly through the twisting maze of stone tunnels that ran under the castle. The soft quiet of the caves was gone, replaced by a pounding, whooshing sound that grew louder with every step they took. A light in the distance beckoned, growing brighter as they walked, sending eerie shadows crawling up the damp rock walls.

Eventually the light was strong enough that Fiona spit on the ball of Glow she had in her hand, discharging the light, and folded the wet lump over itself a few times. Her stomach twisted as she saw a tiny speck of bright red on the Glow. Blood.

She took a deep breath and dumped it back in her pack.

"You couldn't have rubbed it on the wet walls or something?" Rhiannon asked with a disgusted look on her face. "You had to spit on it?"

"No," Fiona said, getting herself under control, "I could've." She winked at the princess. "I just like to spit."

The girls finally turned a corner that emptied them into a wide open space. There were more wooden crates littering the muddy ground, and running through the middle of the cavern was a river of dark water. The sound of rushing water surrounded them, bouncing off the stone walls with such force it was hard to hear themselves think.

And standing on their side of the river, right in front of them, was a monstrously large rat.

It turned and faced them, lifting its head from where it had been drinking. Its whiskers twitched as it sniffed the air and its black eyes glared at the group of newcomers. It stiffened for a minute, seeming to consider its options, then bared its large front teeth and charged.

"AAAAHHH!" Isabel screamed, though the piercing sound was lost in the thunder of the river.

Rhiannon reached for Cricket and Fiona reached for her pack.

Winkle looked at Isabel with her bright lavender eyes and winked, just once. Then she flew toward the cat-sized rat.

The girls watched in horror as a whirl of greenish blue scales tumbled with dirty gray fur. Winkle's eyes glowed red as she battled ferociously with the large rodent. In no time she had him by the throat and was shaking his furry body like a rag doll. But with a swift twist of its thick body the rat escaped her scaly grip. It landed on its feet and rushed straight toward the group of girls, its beady black eyes locked on Isabel.

Isabel screamed again, so loud that the rat faltered, stumbling slightly to the side. Cricket squirmed and fought to be free of Rhiannon's grasp, desperate to get in on the fight.

Winkle scrambled quickly along the floor, coming from behind the rat and grabbed its thick, long tail. She drug it, swinging and writhing, back toward her and the river, away from the girls.

The rodent swung its head around, lightning fast, and connected. Its hard teeth sunk deep into Winkle's scaly flesh. Her gurgling cry of pain echoed through the cavern before it was swept away in the sounds of the running water.

"NO!" Isabel cried.

Winkle lay sprawled in the mud beside the water, her tiny hands clutching where she had been bitten in the neck. The rat stood between her and the group of girls, shaking and breathing hard. It looked back and forth between them, then jumped toward Winkle's injured body.

With one swift motion Winkle rolled to the side and landed a powerful kick to the rat's middle, sending it hurtling into the rushing water. It bobbed up and down a few times as it was carried downstream, before it finally sank to the bottom.

The girls rushed to the water's edge with Isabel in the lead. Winkle managed to sit up, plopping her belly on the ground in front of her. Her semi-webbed fingers pressed tightly against the two gashes in her neck. Blood oozed out from underneath.

"Are you okay?" Isabel asked, getting a closer look at Winkle's neck. "Let me look at that."

"Isabel, don't," Rhiannon cautioned. "She's hurt. You don't know what she'll do."

"Yes I do," Isabel said stubbornly. She reached toward Winkle's neck, carefully lifting her scaly fingers off the bite. The dripping blood glistened against her bright scales, staining Isabel's pale fingers as she gently probed the wounds.

"It's pretty bad," she said, her voice cracking. She looked through her tears at Winkle. "Why did you *do* that?"

Winkle's eyes faded into lavender as she opened her little mouth. "Izz-yy," she gurgled. Then she leaned on the princess and her eyes drifted back to the painful, dark blue.

Fiona stepped forward and crouched down beside them. "Try this." She held out the tin of thistleberry salve. "I don't know if it will work or not, but it's worth a shot."

Isabel took the silver tin and nodded. She carefully spread the reddish goo over Winkle's neck. The slow drizzle of blood coming from her wounds stopped as the salve caked over the holes. She smiled, sighing with relief.

Winkle gasped and wrapped her fingers around Isabel's wrist. "Izz-yy," she croaked.

Isabel cradled the little Cave Bodkin's head in her lap.

"It's okay now," Isabel said, "I think you're going to be okay."

"I don't know," Fiona whispered. Thistleberry salve was an ointment, not a miracle cure.

Isabel wiped Winkle's head, gently caressing the bluish scales. She choked back a sob. There was more blood. And it was going everywhere.

The bite wounds that had been caked shut had started to bleed again.

Winkle gurgled and her eyes fluttered.

"Help her!" Isabel cried. "Do something!"

Fiona ripped the bottom of Rhiannon's dress and quickly tied the fabric around Winkle's neck, hoping to stop the flow.

But it was no use. The fabric turned an ugly shade of red. Winkle was losing too much blood.

"Do something!!" Isabel cried, staring at the others helplessly.

But there was nothing they could do.

"Izz-yy," Winkle whispered for the last time, squeezing Isabel's wrist. Then her scaly fingers went slack and dropped to the muddy ground.

She was gone.

12

The Note

Morning broke on the castle. A bright orange sun rose slowly over the ocean, making the vast expanse of dark water sparkle brilliantly in the new day. A few dolphins jumped and played in the rolling surf, and closer to shore, a group of giant sea turtles rested lazily on the rocks, slowly waking up as they warmed their thick skin in the morning sun.

The King stood in his chambers, staring out the tall windows onto the glorious scene. But he saw none of it. His jaw was clenched and the air burned as it flew through his nose. His hands shook with rage, wrinkling the already tattered piece of paper he held in his grasp. He had no time for nature's beauty this dawn. His eyes saw nothing but the horrors he imagined his girls were suffering.

He had woken early, already thinking of them. He'd worked late into the night with Ferront, both of them eventually falling asleep in the back corner of the library. And he'd not seen his girls to bed. It wasn't something he allowed to happen often, but it did happen.

No one thought of the compromises that came with being King. All anyone saw were the flowing robes and the glittering crown. And, of course, the power. No one saw the look in his daughters' eyes when he didn't have time to read to them, or ride with them. But he knew their disappointment cut deep, and so he'd woken early, thinking of joining them for a big breakfast.

He'd changed clothes in his sleeping room, refreshing his face with a splash of cold water and then dispatched his manservant to call on Rosalie and have her wake the girls and send them to his chambers for an early breakfast in their nightclothes.

He'd walked through his private rooms as he'd headed for his office. The girls would no doubt take some time in rising, he'd thought, and he could still squeeze some work in before breakfast. Perhaps sitting at his desk in the quiet of the morning would help him think of something concerning this wretched mess with Neulock and the fairy. Though he'd doubted it. He and his brother had chewed this one to death last night and still had nothing new.

He'd entered his office and could not believe what he'd seen. Dust and broken pieces of stone littered the ground. One of his chairs was knocked over and the door to his closet was hanging wide open. It looked as if a bomb had gone off, not to mention the smell. There was a burnt, sulphur tinge to the air that put him in mind of explosives.

He'd kicked through the litter of debris on the floor and made his way to his desk. There, laying under a haze of dust, was a note. The handwriting caught his eye. He'd recognized it immediately as Rhiannon's. He'd reached for it, knocking a few books off the cluttered desk in his haste. He'd brushed the dirt from the paper and held it up to read.

Dad,

The fairy is innocent. We're with Fiona Thorn. You have to help us!

His mind had raced. He knew that name. Thorn, Thorn...and then it'd come to him. Fiona Thorn had come before him four years ago, as just a young girl. She'd been accused of killing an entire flock of chickens.

He'd ground his teeth as the memory continued to unravel. The farmer had brought his evidence; a charred mess of feathers and chicken parts he'd stuffed in a potato sack that he carried on his back. The sulphury, singed smell coming from that bag had been awful.

And very similar to the smell that surrounded him right now.

He and Ferront had laughed that day, years ago, after dismissing the girl with a stern warning and sentencing her guardian to a two night stay in the Tower for not being able to pay for the chickens. They'd chuckled, thinking it was lucky they hadn't been caught in half the trouble they'd found as boys.

The girl had seemed a bold and brash youngster who'd just gotten in over her head. He remembered how she'd stood in front of him, proud as you please, without a hint of remorse. She'd actually claimed it was the chicken's fault, flinging her thick braid over her shoulder as she glared at the accusing farmer. She said they'd been too stupid to heed the protection spell that her friend Jaydin had cast in her field, and that they'd wandered uninvited into *her* detonation zone.

Her friend Jaydin.

His eyes darted to the note again. *The Fairy is innocent.*

His hands clenched, crumbling the small piece of paper in his grip.

He turned to the door that led to the common hall. Someone was knocking.

"Yes?" he said brusquely.

Fletcher opened the door and stepped in, his eyes looking everywhere but at the King. Rosalie followed behind, her face full of fear.

"What is it?"

"Sire...the princesses...they are...," Fletcher began.

"They are what, man? Get on with it!"

"They are not in their beds, your majesty," the girls' maidservant said breathlessly. She reached a trembling hand up to her face. "When they didn't come back to their chambers last night, I assumed they were with you..."

The King wasted no more time. "Fletcher, find Graven and Ferront. Bring them to me. Immediately."

Fletcher turned on his heels and ran down the hallway. The sound of anxious pounding on the counselors' doors hung in the air as the King dismissed Rosalie.

He stalked about the office while he waited, angrily kicking the mess that littered his floor, until finally collapsing in the only chair that remained upright. His shoulders slumped and he held his face in his hands, the crumpled note pressed against his distraught face.

"Sire, you have need of me?"

The King rubbed his face and looked up. Graven stood just inside the doorway, his head bowed.

"Graven," he said as he stood, "my daughters are missing."

He ignored Graven's sharp intake of breath and continued, looking straight at the old man. "You are involved in this."

"Sire, I..."

He held his hand up. "We are all involved now." He shook his head and pointed a shaky finger at Graven. "We must put this bickering about the fairy behind us, Graven. You will take your men and find my girls."

"Of course, my liege," Graven said obediently, "but what has happened?" His black eyes narrowed. "What do you suspect?"

"I suspect nothing!" the King shouted. "I know full well what has happened!"

"You do?"

The King shook his fist in the air, the wrinkled edges of the note sticking between his fingers. "It's right here! She's taken them as hostages in exchange for the fairy's release."

Graven's face twitched, fighting to restrain a triumphant smile. "Who your majesty? Who would dare harm the royal princesses?"

"Fiona Thorn." The King's lips curled around the name with distaste as he spit the words at Graven. "This is all you will think of, all you will do. There is nothing but this. It must have your complete attention." The King turned and looked at his trusted counselor. "You will do nothing until you find my girls."

"Rest assured, my liege, I will be thinking of nothing but the princesses."

"Make sure that you do," the King said as he turned to stare numbly out the windows. "And take Ferront with you. The more men I have on this, the better."

"Yes, your majesty," Graven said as he glided toward the door.

"And Graven?" the King said without taking his eyes from the breaking dawn.

"Sire?"

"Start with that demolition master on the coast. McClane."

13

Everfalls

"We can't get across that!" Rhiannon said, throwing her hands up in frustration. "The current is too strong. We'd never make it." She looked back and saw Cricket sitting with Isabel. The little girl was showing her big sister how to work a ball of Glow. "Seriously Fiona, especially with Cricket. We can't cross that."

"I don't want to cross it," Fiona said, "I want to ride it."

"Oh! That's so much better," Rhiannon said. "Are you kidding?"

"No," Fiona answered, stepping toward the wooden crates along the far wall. "I'm not kidding. It's our way out."

With a little luck, and the tarp in her pack, they'd be out of here soon. She didn't know exactly where the river went, but judging from the distance they'd come, they couldn't be far from the ocean. And wherever the river took them, at least it was out of here.

They'd been luckier than she wanted to admit when the Cave Bodkin had handled that rat. Using Blast underground was not a good idea. And without her explosives, things could've gotten ugly. It could've very easily been one of them they'd had to wrap in cloth and eulogize by the river.

~ 78 ~

Fiona walked to Isabel and crouched down beside her. For a minute they were quiet, watching as Cricket played with the ball of Glow.

"How're you doing?"

"I'm okay, I guess," Isabel said, drawing a heart with her finger in the dirt.

She'd taken Winkle's death hard, but seemed comforted as Fiona explained that the little Cave Bodkin had probably saved their lives.

"Does that mean she's a hero?" Isabel asked.

"I think it does," Fiona said, standing up. She walked to Rhiannon and clapped a hand on her shoulder. "Come on! It's been ages since I've been swimming!"

The princess was not amused. "We'll never make it you know. Unless you've got a boat or something in that pack of yours." She raised her eyebrows at Fiona.

"I don't have a boat, exactly..."

"What are you thinking?" Rhiannon asked.

"We'll use those," Fiona said, pointing to the crates along the wall.

"No way," Rhiannon said. "They'll sink. With us in them. Straight to the bottom, like that rat." She looked over her shoulder at Isabel, regretting her choice of words. But her sister was too busy playing with Cricket to have heard.

"I know they'll sink *now,*" Fiona said, smiling, "but not after we get through with them." She swung her pack off her shoulder and dug through until she came out with a wrinkled ball of green fabric.

"We've got this!" she shouted triumphantly, and instantly regretted it, coughing into her hand.

Remember, calm is better. Shouting aggravates things.

She shook out the green ball until it hung flat in front of her.

"How is a poncho going to help?" Rhiannon asked.

"Not just any poncho," Fiona said proudly. "A perfectly, wonderfully water proof poncho."

"Really?" Rhiannon said, tipping her head like she didn't believe a word of it.

"Yep. And if we do make it, you can thank the ladies of Wilma's Hive." Fiona smiled, remembering the first time she'd introduced Jaydin to all of them. They'd swarmed around them, fussing and singing some song about kissing in a tree. She'd wanted to kill them.

"The who?"

"A bunch of bees in the Dappled Forest. Old ladies, mostly." She smiled up at Rhiannon as she smoothed the poncho on the ground. "Queens, really. They lost their hives to younger queens, so now they live together. Come on, help me."

Rhiannon reluctantly got down on her hands and knees and began smoothing the many wrinkles. "And?"

"And I might have brought them a few young honey bees that I found in the Wood, once or twice. And they were grateful."

"For what? The company?"

"No," Fiona laughed, "for the servants."

Rhiannon shook her head. "So they gave you a poncho?"

"No," Fiona explained slowly as they both stood up, "they gave me wax, which I rubbed *into* my poncho." She snapped the fabric beside her, holding it up for inspection. "And now," she said, "it's about as water proof as it gets."

"And you're going to make a boat out of it?" Rhiannon asked, like she was talking to a small child.

Fiona pursed her lips. "I'm going to cut it into pieces and then wrap the pieces around the crates, making three boats out of it."

"And then what?"

"And then we get in the boats."

Rhiannon stared at her in disbelief. "Do you really think it'll work?"

"It has to," Fiona said. "Or we'll drown."

For the next hour the two of them worked together, wrapping the fabric around each crate and securing it at the top with a bit of Fiona's twine, while Isabel played with Cricket.

"Izzy!" Rhiannon called once they'd finished the last one, "Come get your boat!"

****

The girls stood at the river's edge with their wooden boats, such as they were, lined up beside them. The churning water seemed louder than ever as it swept through the cavern.

"Let's do this!" Fiona said, clapping her hands. "Rhiannon, you take Cricket, right?"

"You bet." She waved her arm and her baby sister came toddling over. "Wanna' get in the boat?"

Cricket looked up and nodded. She climbed in the crate and started rocking back and forth, trying to make it move.

"Hang on, hang on," Rhiannon said, shaking her head, "we'll go soon."

"Izzy, you set?" Fiona asked.

But she was gone. Fiona turned and found her along the bank where they'd said goodbye to Winkle. She walked over and put a hand on Isabel's shoulder.

"I know, I know," Isabel said. "Time to go."

She turned and wrapped her arms around Fiona, burying her face in Fiona's chest. "She's a hero, right?" she asked, looking up as her eyes filled with tears.

"Absolutely," Fiona said, surprised at how comfortable she was in the girl's embrace.

"Bye, Winkle." Isabel said, letting go of Fiona. "I'll never forget you."

"None of us will," Fiona said as she led the sobbing princess back to the others.

****

"So, this is it!" Fiona said. She looked at the bedraggled mess they'd all become; dirty, hungry, ripped and scratched. To make it worse, Isabel was tear-stained and still covered in Winkle's blood. Was this what came of spending time with her? No wonder she could count her friends on one hand, with fingers to spare.

"Ready?" she asked, looking at each of them. Regardless of what she'd told them, she knew this was a long shot. That river was raging, and none of them knew where it led. But it was the only shot they had.

She smiled. Despite the rough start, the girls had surprised her. They'd really been pulling their weight. Even Rhiannon. She vowed that somehow she'd see them through this. Frills and all.

Isabel and Rhiannon nodded reluctantly. "Ready."

Cricket had crawled out of her crate to make room for Rhiannon and was bouncing up and down beside Fiona with a huge grin on her face.

Fiona carefully nudged the first crate into the river, steadying it while Rhiannon and Cricket crawled in. It was difficult to balance against the heavy current, but she managed. And when Rhiannon gave her the sign, she let go.

Fiona and Isabel watched as the girls were carried downstream. They rocked a bit on the current, but seemed to be staying afloat.

Rhiannon looked back and gave a thumbs up before rounding the bend and dropping out of sight. And through it all, so loud even the pounding water couldn't silence it, was Cricket's gleeful cry.

"WEEEEE!"

"You're next, Izzy," Fiona said, lightly tapping the next crate. The sound was muffled in the heavy, rushing water.

"And it's safe, right?" Isabel asked as she stepped in. Fiona held the side of the crate as the princess tucked her dirty skirts around her and nestled inside. The crate bobbed up and down in the moving river.

"Do I look like I'd ever do anything unsafe?" Fiona said, laughing.

Isabel's frightened eyes met Fiona's, then she nodded, signaling she was ready. Fiona let go, and she was off, floating on the swift current behind her sisters.

"We're all gonna' die," Fiona mumbled to herself as she grabbed the last crate.

With both hands, she held it behind her, preparing to jump in backwards. She took one last look around the damp cavern, steeled herself against the blow, and fell backward into her crate and the river at the same time.

She landed hard. Her head snapped back, slamming into the top of the wooden crate with a nasty thud that was lost in the roar of the river. Her body slumped as she lost consciousness, leaving her arms and legs hanging over the top like a limp doll. She bounced through the rapids, no more in control of herself than a twig that's tossed about in the pounding surf, riding the waves until it snaps.

****

Up ahead, the princesses were having better luck. Isabel had caught up to her sisters. She floated behind them as the river slowed, winding lazily back and forth through a serpentine in the cavern.

"Hey!" she shouted as she bumped into them.

Cricket stood up and started climbing over Rhiannon, trying to get out of her crate and into Isabel's.

"Not so fast," Rhiannon laughed, brushing her dark, dripping hair out of her eyes. She snatched her little sister by the back of her wet dress. "You have to stay with me, got it?"

Cricket nodded and waved a pudgy, soaked hand at Isabel instead.

"Look!" Isabel shouted over the rushing water, pointing up ahead.

As they rounded a final bend in the cavern the light in the distance became very bright; nearly blinding. Almost at once the sound was deafening, assaulting them with such force they all ducked down and clapped their hands over their ears. The speed of the river began to build and the slope increased, sending them hurtling down a slide of gushing white water.

"AHHHHH!" they cried, though it was impossible to hear over the thunderous crashing of water. They leaned back, bracing themselves as they slid faster and faster down the chute of rushing water.

And then, they were flying.

They shot through the mouth of the falls and for a brief second they were airborne, free of their crates; three princesses tumbling through the air, their grand gowns of fine silks and satins silhouetted against the backdrop of mighty Everfalls, like fancy kites flying on a rainy day.

****

Fiona felt the cold water close around her. She choked and sputtered, waking as her throat filled with salty sea water. She opened her frightened eyes, but couldn't see anything. It was dark; a murky, cloudy green. She was sinking and her lungs were burning. She had to get to the surface. She needed air.

Had she been above water at that moment, she would've seen Rhiannon thrashing in the waves not far behind her. She would've seen how the girl's body was struggling with the weight of her dress, how it was dragging her under like a weighted purple mist.

But Fiona couldn't see anything except the dark ocean closing around her. Her mind was filled with nothing but the air she so desperately needed to live.

Something moved under her and she fought the urge to scream, knowing she would only end up with another mouthful of cold, salty water. She struggled and finally felt herself rising. She clawed hard, fighting for every inch. She could almost taste the clean, crisp air filling her lungs. The surface was getting lighter.

Almost there.

She broke through and gasped. She choked again and coughed as cold salt water flew into her lungs with the air. But it was wonderful. She could breathe.

She pulled herself back, farther away from the crashing falls, her muscles burning as she swam hard against the current.

She held her head barely above the water and scanned the surface. There was no sign of anyone.

She turned around in a circle, fighting to stay afloat while she searched the rough waters for the other girls. She listened closely, trying to hear Isabel crying over the pounding sound of the falls. She searched the cliff face, half expecting to see Cricket climbing it. But it was no use. There was nothing to hear or see other than churning, raging water.

She refused to give up on them, even though she knew it had been too long. They'd drowned, like she nearly had. And it was her fault for dragging them into this. She'd led them through that door. How could she have been so stupid? She'd as good as killed all three princesses of Amryn. And all in just one day. Nice work, even for her.

She struggled as she continued to tread water, but as the tears began to cloud her eyes it became harder to search. She couldn't see anything clearly anymore. In fact, her vision had gotten so bad it looked like there were two giant boulders swimming toward her.

I'm hallucinating. I must be dying.

"Fiona! Thank goodness!" Isabel cried, "There you are! We've been looking everywhere!"

Fiona struggled to tread water and wipe her eyes at the same time, when she felt something under her again. It was large and hard, curved and sort of slippery. She felt it settle under her and then, she was weightless.

She sat on the hard shell and rested, her exhausted muscles thankful for the break. When she finally cleared her eyes, she noticed the back of a large, leathery neck sticking up in front of her. She looked around a few times and saw, to her surprise, that she was sitting on the back of a giant sea turtle.

"Are...you...alright?" a deep voice asked very slowly. It was coming from in front of her.

She blinked a few times, trying to clear her eyes.

Floating in front of her was another giant turtle. He looked like a big oval table floating in the water. His back was brown and covered with bursting orange splotches that repeated on each piece of his shell. The leathery hide of his front flippers was scored with white, making them look like two huge puzzles waving back and forth in the ocean.

The girls were sitting on his back. Isabel in back, her legs hanging over one side, and Cricket up front, leaning forward with her little arms wrapped tightly around the turtle's thick, grayish neck. She was beaming.

And Rhiannon was there too. She rode a smaller turtle who was floating lazily to the left with a slimy hunk of seaweed in his mouth. She was holding a hand up to her forehead, but other than that, she appeared to be fine.

"What?" Fiona asked, coughing and sputtering.

"He asked if you were all right," Isabel said before the turtle had a chance to repeat himself. "He talks kind of slow."

"That...was...some...fall," the turtle said slowly as he blinked, making the brownish yellow crinkles around his eyes snap open and closed.

"I'm okay, now that I found you," Fiona said, trying to catch her breath. She was better now that she could breathe, but still felt a bit woozy. She rubbed the back of her head and found a big, throbbing bump.

"You look awful," Rhiannon said, winking at Fiona.

"Excuse me for not doing my hair," Fiona said. "You don't look so great yourself. What happened?" she asked, relieved to see all of them. She smiled, thinking how hard it was to believe she was this glad to see princesses.

"Don't ask me," Rhiannon said, holding her hands up. "Taking the river was your bright idea."

"They were swimming in the falls," Isabel said, "cleaning the algae from their shells when we flew out the bottom chute. So they helped us. And just in time too." She leaned forward and hugged Cricket. "I couldn't find her anywhere, and then she popped up right in front of me, trying to scramble up on the shell."

"What do you mean 'the bottom chute'?" Fiona said.

"Look." Isabel pointed toward the waterfall.

Fiona looked over her shoulder. A massive cliff face rose behind them, and randomly along its vertical rise were huge openings that gushed torrents of water, all crashing into the ocean.

"That's where the river went?" Fiona said, shaking her head. By the Angels, not a single one of them had any right to be alive. "Not my best plan, if I'm honest."

"Can you take us to the castle?" Rhiannon asked the old turtle. "I need to see my father."

"I don't think that's a good idea," Fiona said. Graven would be watching, they could bet on it. They'd never get to the King unnoticed. Not to mention they had no idea who else was involved. "It might not be so easy to get to him right now, if you know what I mean."

Rhiannon closed her eyes and considered. "Fine," she said, giving in. "Where should we go then?"

Fiona leaned forward and spoke to the old turtle. "Do you know the old farm on the southern coast? The one with the burned barn foundation just beside the ocean?"

"The...one...that...smells...of...gunpowder...half...a...mile...out...to...sea?"

"That's the one!" Fiona said, clapping her hands together. "Take us there. Take me home."

14

McClane & Delia

The smell hit them first.

"What is that?" Isabel asked, holding her nose. She was standing on a large boulder just off the beach, watching the turtles swim back out to sea.

"It's gunpowder," Fiona said, trying to take a deep breath. Her lungs felt half closed though, like someone had stuffed them with cotton. "And redtar sulphur. Isn't it wonderful?" She adjusted her necklace, feeling the bronze key with her fingers. She'd checked a hundred times since they'd come out of the ocean, just to make sure.

Rhiannon walked from the tide pool where Cricket was playing and stood by Fiona. She shielded her eyes from the bright sun and saw an old stone foundation just ahead. Farther up the hill was a small cottage.

"Where are we going?" Isabel asked, jumping down from the boulder.

"There," Fiona said. She pointed up the hill and headed toward the little house.

Rhiannon gathered Cricket, and shaking the tiny crabs and mussels from her little sister's dress, quickly followed Fiona.

"So, is this what smells?" Rhiannon asked as they passed the burned out foundation. The stone walls were held together by crumbling mortar and much of the stone was stained black with the char of an old fire. Nothing stood now but the base of what had once been a barn.

"This one's been out for awhile." Fiona looked at the princess and smirked. "Not as dangerous as it used to be." Her hand trailed lovingly over the rough surface of the wall as she walked by.

"Hey look!" Isabel said, pointing in front of them.

A large yellow dog was running toward them, wagging it's scraggly tail.

"Casey!" Fiona cried, crouching down on her knees. The dog hurled itself into Fiona's outstretched arms, nearly knocking her over. "This is Casey," she said, crawling to her feet. "He's my brother. My hairy dog-brother anyway."

Casey wandered around the group of giggling girls, sniffing and exploring the scents that lingered on their dresses, then shook his head, flapping his great, floppy ears. He ran back to Fiona, anxious to play, but was distracted as a fiery plume of white light shot into the air from behind the cottage. It was followed by a blast of thick, gray smoke that lingered briefly before dispersing on the ocean breeze.

"Looks like he's here," Fiona said, laughing. He won't believe what I've drug home this time.

She looked down and saw Rhiannon and Isabel flat on the ground with their hands over their heads. But Cricket was still standing, looking at the smoke fading in the sky. She must've been adopted, Fiona thought with approval.

"It's just a bit of Angel's Breath," she said, laughing. She shook her head and trotted up the rocky hillside. Casey ran alongside, his pink tongue lolling out the side of his mouth, leaving a heavy trail of drool for the princesses to follow.

Fiona crested the hill and quickly disappeared inside the small stone cottage. Built of mismatched rocks and boulders from the coast, the building's north wall was mostly taken up by a large fireplace. Its slanted roof was a mix of thatched grasses and weeds that were woven through odd pieces of discarded fishing nets that had washed ashore.

In front of the door to the cottage was a clothes line. One end was attached to an unstable, sloping rock wall. And the other was tied to a small, dead tree. The tree looked like it had died prematurely, judging by its lack of leaves and the crispy, burnt edges on its branches.

"I guess we go in?" Isabel said as she ducked under the trousers that hung on the line. She reached back and held them up for Rhiannon. "Should we knock?"

Rhiannon grabbed Cricket, who was flapping her arms through the hanging pants. "I guess," she said. Her face twisted in disapproval at the black char marks on the bottom of the wooden door.

Isabel raised her hand to knock, but the door swung inward first.

"I thought you were right behind me," Fiona said, catching her breath. She stepped back to make room and almost tripped on Casey. He was behind her, wagging his tail excitedly.

The cottage was small, with only two rooms. The main room was the largest and in it, close to the fireplace, were two wooden chairs and a table. The table was small and bare, except for a rusting can full of sea grasses.

Other than the table, every bit of space was covered. Along one wall was a bookshelf bursting with fabrics of all kinds. They were organized by color, their range spanning the entire spectrum, making it seem like someone had painted a richly decorated rainbow on the wall.

An unfinished dress in luxurious green velvet was draped over a ladder beside the shelf. And under the ladder was an open box full of sewing supplies; needles, scissors and thread of every color.

There were piles of books everywhere on the hard-packed dirt floor, some reaching waist high, and crates full of all sorts of things with fuses coming out of them. One crate was full of nothing but inactive wads of Glow.

In the fireplace, a big iron pot hung above a bed of smoldering coals, sending a delicious smell of roasted chicken, wild onions and potatoes into the air.

"That smells really good," Isabel said as she stepped inside. Her stomach growled loudly. "Sorry." She looked at Fiona and shrugged her shoulders. "I'm starving."

"Don't worry," Fiona said as they came in. "Dee just went out back for a second. When she comes in, you won't be able to stop her from feeding us."

"I would hope so," Rhiannon said, combing her hair with her fingers. "It's not every day actual royalty crosses your threshold."

"Would you like to cross it again?" Fiona asked, raising her eyebrows and gesturing toward the door.

"You're right," Rhiannon mumbled. "I apologize."

Fiona walked to the fireplace and lifted the lid from the pot. A wave of salty, savory goodness spread through the room. It was almost too much for such hungry girls to bear. The heavy lid clanged pleasantly when she put it back on the simmering pot.

She adjusted a stack of books into chair height and was about to sit, when she noticed Cricket, diving head first into a crate. Fiona pulled her up by her feet. The little girl dangled upside down, both hands gripping fistfuls of the moldable white explosive she'd found.

"I'll take that!" Fiona said, easing two huge hunks of Blast from her hands. "We're going to have to keep an eye on you!" she said, laughing as Cricket began toddling around the small room full of dangers.

"Here," she said, dragging an entire crate of Glow into the center of the room. "You can play with this." Cricket sat down in front of the crate and smiled.

"Grab a pile of books or something and sit down," Fiona said, looking at the other two. This was surely the first time they'd heard that. "Just don't sit on anything with a fuse," she added, glancing around. She looked at the wads of Blast in her hands. "Or anything soft and gushy." She would've paid much to save the looks on their faces. "Yeah, so, only sit on books."

"You don't have to sit on books!" a cheery woman's voice said as she came bustling through the door. "My gracious, we have a big, long bench here somewhere." She was small and round and very busy. She stepped into the room, carefully avoiding Cricket, who was almost buried inside the crate of Glow, and whirled through the small cottage, moving and rearranging things until she found what she was looking for.

"Here," she said, gesturing to the bench she'd uncovered, as she faced her company for the first time.

"Miss Delia!" Isabel shouted.

"Well hello, child!" Delia said with a big smile. "Fiona said she brought company, but I didn't expect this."

She reached for Isabel's hands. "I am so relieved to see you girls! We've been so worried. My gracious! But what has happened to these dresses?" She twirled Isabel around in a slow circle, examining the drenched gown.

"Both of you!" she said, giving Rhiannon's dirty wet dress the same scrutiny. She clucked her tongue and turned to Fiona. "I suppose the baby is wet too?"

"Dee, we were locked in a storage room and left for dead, shot out the bottom of Everfalls and been swimming with sea turtles all morning. Yeah, we're all pretty wet."

"Sea turtles, huh?" a gruff voice asked. Fiona looked past Delia at the big man hunched in the doorway. His thinning gray hair was pulled back in a low ponytail, exposing a weathered face covered in dark stubble. He looked at the princesses and smiled warmly, then glanced at Fiona and winked. His pale blue eyes sparkled with mischief.

"McClane!" Fiona shouted. She threw herself into his big arms, causing Casey to raise his head from where he was laying in front of Cricket.

McClane hugged Fiona, then held her at arms' length, gripping her shoulders as she coughed. "What sort of trouble are ye in, girl?" He squinted and blew a loose strand of hair out of his face.

"What makes you say that?" Fiona rolled her eyes and caught her breath. She sat back down on her stack of books, coughing into her hand.

"'Cause ye look like hammered tar, fer one," he said.

"It's nothing," Fiona said, shaking her head. "Just a summer cold."

"But you said...," Isabel began, but stopped as Fiona glared at her.

McClane lumbered to the older princesses. He stretched his bear paw hand out to them. "I'm McClane," he said, "glad to meet ye' both."

Rhiannon stood and curtsied.

As Isabel shook McClane's rough hand, her eyes became huge.

McClane held his hand up, turning it back and forth as he examined it. "What'd ya' do with me finger?"

The sisters looked at each other, confused. His pinky finger was missing.

"Lost that wee 'an long ago," he said with a chuckle, nodding to himself. His eyes flitted to the princesses and he grinned.

"But this 'an," he said as he swept his other hand from behind his back, holding his index finger in front of them, "is only a year or so gone. Still tingles like the tip is really there." He wiggled the stumpy finger at them.

"EEOOUU!!" Isabel screamed.

The room erupted in laughter.

"See there," he said, smiling at Isabel, "it just takes some gettin' used to."

He walked toward the fireplace and stopped next to the crate of Glow to pet Casey. Cricket had pasted herself from head to toe in the sticky, luminescent material. She stood in the center of the crate, looking up at McClane like a giant, bright yellow glow worm.

He squatted down on his big haunches and looked her in the eye. She stared back until he finally burst out laughing and stood up, shaking his head. "Don't believe we ever had 'an that small 'round here," he said as he grabbed one of the wooden chairs. He swung it around and sat down.

Delia ushered Rhiannon and Isabel to the long bench and dished out heaping bowls of chicken and potatoes to everyone. Once they were all eating, she settled by the table and blew gently on her own steaming bowl of stew.

"So, Fiona Eloise," McClane asked through a mouthful, "what is goin' on?"

Rhiannon nearly choked on her chicken. She sputtered and coughed. "Fiona *Eloise?*"

"Leave it alone," Fee said, glaring. They may have made some strides toward friendship, but this was out of the question. Not even Jaydin used her middle name.

"What've ye done," McClane cut in, "that has the King's men knockin' on me door at first light this morning?"

All the girls, except for Cricket, who was sitting on Delia's lap, glowing and chewing her third drumstick, stared, open mouthed at McClane.

"WHAT?" Fiona blurted. "Who was here?"

"Did my father come?" Rhiannon asked anxiously.

"Why would they come here?" Isabel wondered.

"We don't know why, child," Delia said, glancing at all of the girls protectively. "We were hoping you could tell us."

With a greasy hand Cricket plopped the ruins of her gnawed chicken bone into Delia's bowl. She hopped down and wandered over to Casey, who began licking her hands and face with his big, sloppy tongue.

"What happened? Who came?" Fiona asked as she started pacing around the room.

"It was that weasel Graven and," McClane said, nodding to the sisters, "your Uncle Ferront. They both had at least ten of their own men. Looked like a carnival out here, what with all the fancy banners waving in the breeze." He brought his big hands to his hips. "And Fiona, look at me."

She stopped pacing and met his gaze. "They're after you," he said. "They think you kidnapped the princesses."

"WHAT??"

"That's crazy," Rhiannon said, shaking her head. "It's a trick. It has to be. It's Graven again. I mean," she looked at Fiona and smiled, "I left a note for my father. I left it right on his desk. I said very clearly that the fairy was innocent, that we were with you and that we needed help."

Fiona's shoulders slumped and she let out a long sigh. "You said you were with me? You used *my name*?"

"Yes, actually, I did."

"It's just that," Fiona began, plopping heavily down on her stack of books, "the King and I," she continued, holding the palm of her hand up to her forehead, "we don't exactly..."

"Yer Da' knows Fiona," McClane said, "from years ago, when she was about yer age." He scratched his thick fingers on his chin. "We was summoned, the two of us, fer a crime. She was only 'bout this tall," he said proudly, holding his hand a little above his waist, "but she stood in front of the King hisself and told him what was what."

He looked at Delia. "We explained it, din't we? Went through the whole thing, with that grubby farmer and his sack of feathers leering at her the whole time. He was lucky the law was there or I woulda'..."

"Mickey," Delia soothed, "the man lost an entire flock of chickens."

"You know it wasn't my fault! Jaydin set the protection spell!" Fiona shouted. "How was I supposed to know they would be too stupid to figure it out?"

"You killed chickens?" Rhiannon asked.

"Not on purpose," Fiona said, rolling her eyes, "which I told your father. But he wouldn't listen. And McClane," she said, gesturing to the big man, "had to spend two nights in the Tower."

"But you don't get locked up for something like that," Rhiannon said, confused. "You must be mistaken. Father wouldn't do that."

"It's no mistake, Miss," McClane said, raising his head proudly. "I couldn't pay and spent the time to prove it." He smiled. "But it weren't no hardship. Me and Bo, the master jailor, go way back."

"No one's blaming you, Fiona," Delia said soothingly. "We know it was an accident." She leaned back in her chair. "Besides, it sounds like you've got other things to worry about now."

"I have to find Manzy," Fee muttered to herself.

"Not so fast," McClane said, "Ye still haven't told me what's going on."

"It's Graven. He's after Jaydin and the King." Fiona began pacing the small cottage again. Her breath was short, making a light whistling sound as she huffed. "And now us. Plus," she said hesitantly, looking at the floor, "I saw who cursed the boy."

"By the Angels, Fiona!" McClane bellowed, "did ye' tell the King? They're 'bout to hang that youngin', I saw the scaffold meself when I was in town yesterday. A hateful, ugly thing, it was."

"I tried," she said, gesturing to the princesses, "but we ran into trouble before I could find him."

"But no one was there that day, dear, save Jaydin and Neulock," Delia said. "Everyone knows that. How could you know what happened?"

Fiona scuffed her foot in the smooth dirt floor. "I looked in the waters."

McClane's eyes widened, like two great white saucers. He stood and caught Fiona by the shoulders. "Tell me ye' din't." He shook her. "Tell me!"

Delia covered her face in her hands and wept.

Fiona hung limp against the big man's anger until he pulled her close and held her. "What do ye owe?"

"I don't know," Fiona mumbled. "I threw some Dragon's Tongue and willow root into the water, but it doesn't seem to have been enough."

"A summer cold," Delia whispered, shaking her head. "Indeed." She walked to the shelf full of fabric and began digging behind the reds. "Here," she said, heading toward Fiona, "this might help." She held a plump fruit in front of her. It was round and reddish orange with a rough outer rind.

"Ulli fruit," Fiona said, taking it from Dee. "I should've thought of that. Thanks." She tossed it into the air, then made a face as she peeled the rough rind. The smell was terrible, like a dead animal rotting in a pile of manure.

Both princesses covered their noses, disgusted with the smell.

"You think that's bad," Fiona said, grimacing as she choked down the last of the bright red fruit segments, "it tastes even worse."

"It's no cure," McClane grumbled, pointing a disapproving finger at Fiona, "but it might help. 'Spose to be good for the winds."

Fiona stood and took a breath. She still felt like someone was standing on her chest, but she wasn't wheezing anymore.

"Well, ye just missed Manzy," McClane said. "She showed up late last night looking for ye. Said there'd been a bit of trouble at the castle, but wouldn't get into it. Dee and I din't get worried, really, 'til the King's men rode up this morn."

He rubbed his hands down his dirty trousers and stood up. "She stayed all night waiting for ye, and hid out in the barn when the men came."

"Was there a big snake with her? And did she say where she was going?" Isabel asked.

"I din't see no snake," McClane said. "Where she's headed, I couldn't say."

"I know where she's going," Fiona said. "She won't have to wait long."

"Wait where? What are you talking about?" Rhiannon asked.

"McClane," Fiona said, ignoring Rhiannon, "I have to go. I don't have much time."

"I know it," he answered, rubbing his face in his hands. "Come on, let's get ye set." He wrapped an arm around her shoulder and smiled. "Where's yer pack? I've some new lovelies fer ye."

"I lost it," she said, hanging her head, "in the sea."

****

A few hours later they stood together, this strange group of bedraggled royalty and grufty demolition experts, gathered outside the cottage. The girls were dressed now, after spending the afternoon in burlap sacks as Delia dried their clothes by the fire. For Fiona, seeing Rhiannon in a burlap sack had almost made the whole thing worthwhile.

"I still think you should go home," Delia said, looking at the princesses. She rubbed her hand over Cricket's wispy hair. "I know your lady mother would be worried."

"But we can't, Miss Delia," Isabel answered.

"And why not, child?"

"Because we don't know who else is working with Graven," Rhiannon cut in. "We could end up right back in that room full of rats before any of us could even say Shadowbells."

"Or worse," Fiona said.

"Are ye good 'n stocked?" McClane asked, kicking up a tiny cloud of dust as he fidgeted with his feet.

Fiona patted her freshly loaded pack. After hearing their plan to travel to the Enchanted Wood, McClane had outfitted them with supplies fit for a castle full of knights. Each of them, including Cricket, was hauling gear now. They had canvas bags strapped to their backs, loaded with canteens of water and dried food, including another bunch of Ulli fruit for Fiona. He'd included small knives for the older girls and promised Cricket, in complete sincerity, that she could have one the next time she came.

He'd refilled Fiona's pack with Smoker balls and blocks of Blast, among other things. Strangely, he was fresh out of Glow, but he gave them each two new candles to stuff into their already heavy bags.

~ 97 ~

"I think we're set," Fiona said, laughing. She was breathing easier now. The Ulli fruit seemed to be working. "We'll be lucky to get half a mile down the road carrying all this."

"There's one more thing I have fer ye." He turned and walked behind the cottage. He came back carrying a massive bundle, covered in a large piece of burlap. He smiled and winked. "If ye think ye can carry it."

The girls watched, like it was Savior's Day morning, as he lifted the burlap. He uncovered four small crossbows.

"I know they're small," he said as he handed them out, "but they're special. They're Hazard Bows. And they're beauties."

He pointed to the arrow as Fiona examined hers.

"The tips explode." He smiled proudly, his eyes gleaming with the possibilities. "And," he said, touching the one he'd made for Cricket, "this one just explodes in a ball of fire." He looked at Rhiannon, waiting for her approval. "No gunpowder or pieces a' glass like the others. Safety first!"

Rhiannon looked at him and shook her head. She was speechless.

If I'd known it was that easy to shut her up, Fiona thought, I'd have given Cricket a deadly weapon yesterday.

"Here, Mick," she said quickly, "I'll just hang onto hers, ya' know, until she needs it."

"Yeah, alright," he said. He looked at Fiona and took a deep breath. "Ask Caelia, now. She'll know." He hugged her again. "She'll know what you owe."

"I will," Fiona said, hugging him back. She closed her eyes and breathed him in; clean sweat, dust, redtar, gunpowder, and tried not to think that this could be the last time she'd see him.

****

"So," Rhiannon said, looking back toward the cottage as they crested the first hill, "what was that about? I thought you were a Bright Eye or something, with no human parents. I pictured a cave littered with skulls and stuff."

Fiona laughed. "Very funny." She smiled and inhaled the damp, burnt smell of home. "It's a long story."

~ 98 ~

"Well, we have plenty of time," Rhiannon said, swinging her Hazard Bow at her side. Her heavy canvas pack hung on her back above her purple skirts, making her look like the fugitive princess she'd become. "And while you're at it, please explain how you thought the Moonshadow was a good idea."

Fiona opened her mouth, about to explain; about how she and Manzy had been raised together, paired in a beautiful ceremony on their Matching Day thirteen years ago, about how she came to know McClane and Delia some years after that, and even about the desperation that had led her to the Moonshadow. But she was cut off by a humongous noise.

KABOOOOOM!

They all ducked, and when they stood up they saw a cloud of grass, dirt, rock and dust falling through the air on the hillside below the cottage.

"He's loud," Isabel shouted as she trotted ahead to the older girls. "But I like him." Cricket trailed behind, playing with a big stick she'd picked up along the way.

"Fiona," Rhiannon said, "I was thinking..."

Don't hurt yourself, Fiona thought. "And?"

"With Graven chasing us, well, you for kidnapping us, that ought to buy Jaydin and Father more time, right? We'll keep that old slug too busy to hurt anyone." Rhiannon fluffed her skirt. "Isn't that good news?"

"My best friend is about to be hanged for a crime he didn't commit, I'm slowly dying from my reckless attempt to save him, the only thing stalling the process tastes like a stinking worm turd, and now I'm being hunted for kidnapping?" Fiona raised her eyebrows at the princess. "Yeah, great news."

15

Old Friends

The door swung open and slammed against the stone wall. Jaydin wasn't surprised that someone was there; he'd heard them coming. Their thunderous stomping had echoed so loudly on the stone walls as they'd climbed the winding stairs of the Tower that he was already standing, anticipating the arrival. What did surprise him was who was there.

"Your Majesty," he said nervously, tipping his head.

Was he here to release him? Or had he decided to give in to the mounting pressure of his accusers? It could only be one or the other, Jaydin thought, his stomach twisting in knots. Freedom or death.

The King stood in the doorway, in front of the jailor. His face was flushed, more from a raging anger than the brisk walk up the steps. He was dressed casually for a king, wearing only a cotton tunic and trousers. His pants were tucked into leather knee-high boots that laced up the fronts. But around his waist was a magnificently tooled leather belt, an extravagance of craftsmanship that only the very wealthy could afford. And hanging from his fancy belt was a sword. It was the rounded, well worn end of the hilt, so dangerously within reach of the King's shaking fist, that grabbed Jaydin's attention.

"Don't 'Your Majesty' me, boy!" he said, quickly coming face to face with Jaydin. "I want the meaning of this," and he shoved his palm into Jaydin's chest, pinning a piece of paper between them. "And I want it now."

Jaydin's heart hammered, caught off guard by the sudden attack. His eyes flashed to Bo, who was still standing in the doorway. The jailor shrugged his shoulders. There was nothing he could do.

"You'll get no help from him, boy!" the King said. "This is between you and me. Explain it."

Jaydin took the rumpled piece of paper. His trembling hands made the ivy tattoo that twisted around his right arm look like it was blowing in the breeze.

Dad,

The fairy is innocent. We're with Fiona Thorn.
You have to help us!

"Sir," he began, shaking his head, "I don't understand. I...I don't know anything about this."

The King snatched the note and grabbed Jaydin by the arm. He drug him to the closest wall, nearly snapping his wing as the tip snagged on the ceiling. He slammed the note against the stone and began smoothing it out.

"Look at it again," he said, grabbing Jaydin by the back of the head. He pushed his face against the wall, smashing it into the note. "My daughters are missing. With nothing left behind but this note!" He pushed hard on the back of Jaydin's head, then let go. The note fluttered to the ground.

Jaydin bent down and picked it up. He stood, his back sweating against the stone wall and watched the King pace furiously around the small room, following the same path he'd used for the past two turns.

"I don't know where they are," he said. His voice cracked despite his best attempt at bravery. "I didn't even know they were gone."

"Maybe not," the King said, stopping in front of Jaydin. "But you do know Fiona Thorn."

Jaydin recoiled as the man said her name; he'd spit the words like he was trying to rid himself of a sour taste.

"Yes," Jaydin said.

There'd been times over the years when being friends with Fiona had come at a price. Like when McClane first taught her to use Angel's Breath. It's white hot blast of explosive fury was tricky to master, and at seven her blasting technique had still been a bit scattered. She'd burnt down more of his favorite tree houses and singed his wings with that stuff more times than he could count. Before she had it down, being her friend was nothing short of dangerous.

But this was way worse.

"Tell me where she's taken them. Now!" the King bellowed, his deep voice echoing around the small room.

"You think Fiona has taken your daughters?"

"Don't toy with me, boy," the King said, stepping closer, his eyes focused on Jaydin. "This is no time for your fairy silliness. My girls are in danger, and if you have any wish to see the morning, you'll tell me what she's done with them."

Jaydin shuffled his feet and looked again at the note, eager to get away from the King's piercing stare. "But sir, Fiona wouldn't take your children."

The King's eyes widened, and the boy paused, unsure of his answer. He decided to risk it and go with the truth. "She may be a lot of things, sir, but a kidnapper isn't one of them. She would never hurt anyone."

"You forget, boy," the King said with raised eyebrows, "I know Miss Thorn a little myself," he smirked, "and hurting things is exactly what she does."

"That's not true! Not innocent things, anyway," Jaydin said. "At least, never on purpose." He shook his head, remembering how, at nine, she'd been heartbroken for days after killing an entire nest of red-bellied wren eggs.

They'd been running through the Wood that day, playing hide and seek with a little flickerfawn while Manzy napped in the sun. And he'd teased her. For some reason he'd stuck his tongue out and called her a weak little girl. Why he'd ever said such a thing, especially to her, he couldn't imagine. But he had, and she'd wasted no time coming after him.

He'd laughed at her blind fury, he remembered, and had taken off into the air, never shy about using his magical advantage. He'd glided easily to the top branches of the milkwood tree and sat there smiling, sticking his tongue out, taunting her and waving. She'd looked a lot like the King that day, he thought sourly, remembering how her face had turned red with rage and humiliation.

She'd followed him, climbing to the top of the tree without hesitation, cursing and threatening him the whole way. Only when she'd accidentally knocked the nest of eggs from one of the upper branches had the game changed.

She'd reached out, in a desperate attempt to grab the nest, and lost her balance. There'd been no time to catch her, or the eggs. He'd flown as fast as he could, diving through the air, but couldn't get there in time. The eggs landed hard, smashing all over the ground, their little lives over before they'd even begun. Fiona had been luckier, ending up with only a badly broken wrist. But even after he'd flown her back to the Hollow where his mother had healed her, she'd wailed for days over the lost babies.

The King grabbed Jaydin by the front of his shirt and shoved him against the wall. "I've seen her accidents, boy!" His breath was hot against Jaydin's face. "Up close and personal. And I swear, if you..."

"Your Majesty!" Bo called from the doorway, "was that your brother I heard riding outside?" The man stood firm as he interrupted his sovereign, supported by the sturdy doorframe he leaned on and his strong belief in the fair treatment of his prisoners. "Perhaps he has news of the princesses?"

The King loosened his fingers from Jaydin's shirt. He took a deep breath, regaining his composure. He released the boy, turned on his heels and walked swiftly toward the door.

"Mark my words," he said to Jaydin, though he was staring at Bo, "if she hurts my girls, you'll be the first to pay the price. Understood?" And before either of them could answer, he pushed past the old jailor and ran down the winding steps.

16

Annis

Manzy shook her head, trying to itch the strange tickle on her neck. She was resting in the grass with her legs tucked neatly in front of her. She tossed her head up and down, and shook once more for good measure.

Something dashed in front of her face.

"You almost made me sick!" The voice rang in the air like little bells. It was coming from a tiny fairy, hovering above her.

He huffed angrily and was gone, flitting toward the pond. He lit upon the edge, dipping his delicate copper wings into the water.

"What was that about?" Kevin asked as he slid through the grass, stopping by Manzy.

"Nothing," she laughed, "just a dragonfly fairy that ended up in my mane." She looked down at Kevin and smiled. "Clearly it was my fault."

He laughed and coiled himself in front of her, basking in the sunlight. He closed his eyes and sighed as the warm sun melted into his scales, blanketing him with its delightful, soothing heat.

Manzy lowered her head. "Speaking of fault," she began, "was that you yesterday on the Plains? Chasing that rat?"

Kevin lazily opened one eye, his long lashes fluttering. "What?"

"You know what." She lowered her head until they were almost eye to eye. "Was that you who ran in front of Midnight yesterday afternoon?"

He closed his eye and nestled into his coils. "Yes," he said. "It was me. I just haven't had a chance to properly apologize to Isabel."

Manzy glanced at the pond. The dragonfly fairy was gone, perhaps in search of more mischief. She watched the smooth water of the Moonshadow sparkle brilliantly, the afternoon sunlight bouncing on its surface like little dancing sprites.

"Hopefully you'll get that chance soon," she said. "If we don't see them by tomorrow, I'm going to be more than worried."

"I will be most anxious as well." He lifted his head and looked at her. "Will she be terribly upset?"

"She'll be furious," Manzy said, smiling despite her fears. "But she'll get over it."

"I was nearly starving, and as I explained before..."

"Not Isabel," Manzy said. "I thought you meant Fiona. When she finds out I told Caelia she used the Moonshadow's magic, she's going to blow a fuse."

"You were just worried."

"I still am." She stretched her neck. "But without knowing what Fiona had in her heart when she struck the bargain, Caelia can't know how to pay the debt. Without Fiona, there's nothing she can do."

"I've never known anyone to do such a thing," Kevin said. "Fiona's very brave."

"And very stupid," Manzy said. She snorted, blowing pollen into the air. "I figured as a spy you'd of seen it all."

"I know of the Moonshadow's magic, of course," he said, "and of its calming properties. I tell you," he said, stretching his body along the warm grass, "I haven't felt this relaxed since the time I was lulled, quite by accident, into a two day trance by the harmonies of the Ringing Trees. But never have I seen something so selfless as what Fiona did for the fairy."

"Humph," Manzy snorted, "Reckless and foolish, more like it."

Kevin rolled his eyes.

"You never told me you'd been so far north as the Ringing Trees," Manzy said, changing the subject. "Lindley set out for there last Spring."

The two old friends spent the rest of the afternoon on the banks of the pond. Kevin slithered off in search of food while Manzy napped, and when he returned, his stomach vaguely shaped of rodent, he curled up beside her and napped too. They rested quietly for awhile, recovering from their long journey that morning. And when the sun slowly began to set, chilling the air as its pink-orange glow sunk in the sky, they talked some more.

They spoke of many things; of interesting places they'd seen since the last time they'd been together, and of the grand party planned for tonight in the Wood. An elder's time of Shine had arrived and the whole Wood was buzzing with excitement.

But what they never mentioned were the girls. They didn't talk about where they could be or what could be taking them so long. They didn't talk about Graven and Ferront showing up at the cottage on the coast, or just how unlikely it was that four young girls could escape the notice of trained King's men on horseback. They didn't talk about how news of Jaydin's impending hanging was everywhere, or how every minute that passed meant Fiona's time was running out.

They didn't speak of these things because they were both very afraid.

The sky was completely dark by the time they decided to leave the pond and wander back for the party. They'd crested the small hill that surrounded the Moonshadow and were crossing the clearing back toward the Wood when a small bright light flew out of the trees.

"You're to follow me!" he said, floating in front of Manzy. He looked like a bright white spark, shouting instructions. "At once!"

The fairy led them through the forest, bouncing like a tiny fallen star, until they stood before a massive tree. It was very old, and larger than any other. It had a large hollow at the base, fitted with a wooden door. The top of the door was arched, carved to fit the ancient tree, and the bottom was covered in soft moss.

"Thank you," Manzy said as the tiny sprite gestured for them to enter.

She nudged the door with her head and stepped through. The room was round and very big. A muted yellow light glowed inside as thousands of lightning bugs rested on the walls, blinking and crawling around. Their soft light followed the shape of the hollow, making the room look like an upside down funnel, lit from within.

Poking through the haze of glowing bugs were small ferns and toad lilies. Their small roots spread along the inside wall, reaching into the room with their delicate life, giving the impression of being outside in the forest.

Caelia was on the far side of the room, sitting in a smooth wooden chair that had been carved specially for her. It allowed her to sit comfortably, with her wings spread behind her, as most fairies preferred.

"Ahh, Manzanita Rose," she said warmly as they entered, "come in please."

The lilting sound of Caelia's voice was nearly as soothing as the Moonshadow. Manzy instantly felt at ease. "It's good to see you again, Caelia," she said, stepping into the room. She walked lightly at first, adjusting to the squishy texture of the mossy floor. "I'd like to introduce an old friend of mine."

She looked down and saw Kevin smiling broadly.

"Pleased to make your acquaintance," he said, batting his luxurious lashes at the fairy queen. "My name is Charles Ebeneezer Fitzpatrick the Third. But my friends call me Kevin."

Caelia leaned forward in her grand chair. "Welcome, Kevin. A friend of Manzanita's is a friend of the Wood. Please, come in."

As they walked they passed a stone table tucked into a small nook on the right. Around the table were the biggest toadstools Manzy had ever seen, reaching almost to her knees. They were new since the last time she'd been here, and judging by the faint blue glitter that surrounded them, they were enchanted. Peeking from behind one of them was a pair of blue eyes, shining brighter than any magic's glow.

"AKE! AKE!" Cricket cried. She shot into the room, lunging for Kevin.

"Princess!" he shouted, his black and yellow eyes flashing. He swept toward Cricket, dashing around her with glee. She laughed and squealed as he squeezed her tight.

~ 107 ~

"By the Angels!" Manzy said, delighted. "Are they all here?"

"Yes," Rhiannon said, popping her head from behind a screen of ferns to the left, "we're all here." She put her hands on her hips and looked impatiently at Isabel, who was sitting on the floor below. "But Izzy's hurt. We're waiting for Fiona to get back with more thistleberry."

"It's not my fault my knee is the size of your big head," Isabel said.

"What in the world happened?" Manzy asked, trotting toward them.

"I tripped on a rock," Isabel began.

Rhiannon rolled her eyes. "I don't think she was talking about your knee."

"The girls have had quite an adventure," Caelia said, smiling. "And while they did come hobbling into the Wood, struggling to carry the injured princess between them, I think they're alright now." She glanced at Manzy. "Barely."

"And Fiona?" Manzy asked.

"Here as well," Caelia answered more seriously. "She's doing remarkably well, considering. I sent her for more thistleberry. She should be back soon."

"And the debt?" Manzy asked. "Did you figure out what she owes?"

"Yes," Caelia began. "But Manzy..."

"She didn't kidnap you, did she?" Manzy asked the girls, laughing with relief now that Caelia knew how to save Fiona's life.

"As if," a sarcastic voice said from behind them. Fiona walked through the door, carrying an armload of brambles and berries. She nudged the door closed with her boot.

"There you are," Manzy said, trotting toward Fiona. She nestled her muzzle into Fiona's chest as Fiona gently rubbed her ears.

"What took you so long?" Fiona said with a smirk, placing the pile of thistleberry brambles on the table.

"You seem great," Manzy said, looking Fiona up and down. "Did you already settle the debt?"

"I wish," Fiona said. "Delia gave me some Ulli fruit. I've been eating one every few hours." The truth was they tasted so bad she'd almost rather have her wheezing cough back. Almost.

Caelia flew forward and gathered the thistleberries from the branches. She crushed them and headed toward Isabel.

"I just finished the last one though," Fiona said, making a face. "So we'd better think of something else." She brushed the dirt from the front of her vest.

"Well, what's owed?" Manzy asked happily. "A barrel of blood honey? Ten measures of wooly rosemary? A feathering branch from the Rowan Oak? By Heaven's Gate, let's get done with it and put the whole thing behind us. Tell me what it is. I'll get it right now."

"Manzy," Fiona began, her eyes flashing at Caelia, "it's not that simple."

"Of course it is. You struck a bargain," Manzy said, nodding her head. "Now that we know what you owe, you'll pay it. And you'll be fine."

Caelia finished with Isabel's knee and flew toward Manzy. "She owes a life, Manzy."

"What?" Manzy looked from Caelia to Fiona and back. "But why?"

Caelia laid a hand on Manzy's neck. "In her heart, she wished for knowledge that would save Jaydin's life. Only another life will be counted as payment."

"That's ridiculous!" Kevin shouted, slithering forward. "How could anyone pay such a price?"

"I haven't figured that out yet," Caelia admitted.

Fiona shook her head. "Me either."

Manzy looked like she'd been kicked in the stomach.

For Fiona, it was unbearable. Being the cause of that much pain was worse than knowing she might die. She forced herself to smile. "Don't worry. We'll think of something," she said, nudging Manzy. "Judging by how things were moving before, I have at least another day or two before it gets really bad."

"Another day!" Manzy shouted, pacing the small room. "By the Angels, Fiona Thorn, I will not lose my life's match in *another day or two*."

"Then we'd better figure out who that old woman is," Fiona said. "She's the key."

"What?" Rhiannon asked, stepping away from Isabel.

"I saw an old woman in the Moonshadow. I don't know what to make of it though."

"What, exactly," Caelia said, "did you see?"

"I saw an old woman covered in ice. And she was standing by a big pot, gripping a Sarastro with...claws. I think she's responsible for cursing the boy."

Caelia's eyes flashed. "Did you say claws?"

"Yeah," Fiona said. "Weird, right? But I swear she had big ugly claws, with iron talons for fingers."

"Heaven's Gate," Caelia said, slumping in her chair, "she's made a Sarastro."

"Caelia," Manzy said, trotting toward the fairy queen, "what is it?"

"Yes, my lady," Kevin said, "you look as if you've seen a ghost."

Caelia took a deep breath and sat up. "Many years ago, when I was just a young fairy, I had a friend named Annis." She closed her eyes, remembering. "She was beautiful and bright and we were together always. Until Lindley."

"Jaydin's father?" Fiona asked.

"She was in love with him. It didn't matter that I'd seen him first, or that we were perfectly happy together." Caelia shook her head, pleading the old case. "Or that he never thought of Annis that way."

She shrugged her shoulders, her wing tips bobbing behind her. "But I was young and it was tearing our friendship apart. So I promised to never see him again." She sighed. "But in my heart I still loved him." She threw her arms into the air. "I wanted her to tell me it was alright, to say she understood, to free us from her guilt."

All eyes were glued to Caelia, hanging on her every word.

She leaned back in her chair, defeated. "But she didn't. She followed us through the Wood, making sure we stayed apart, holding me to my promise. And though he pleaded and told her he loved only me, she wouldn't relent." Her eyes grew hard and dark. "She said if she couldn't have him, neither could I."

She nodded to herself. "We kept to the bargain for over a season, until the day Lindley asked me to stay by his side forever, to be his mate."

Isabel elbowed Rhiannon. "Did he ask you to marry him?" Rhiannon made a face and shushed her.

Caelia smiled, despite the pain that wrapped the memory. "Yes, child. We walked to a beautiful meadow on the outskirts of the Wood, and there, as we sat holding hands in an old maple tree, he asked me."

"And?" Isabel asked eagerly, leaning forward.

"I said yes," Caelia said.

Isabel clapped. "I just knew it!"

"Fiona just said he was Jaydin's father," Rhiannon said, shaking her head. "It's not exactly a mystery."

"But what about Annis?" Fiona asked, still waiting to know how any of this could help.

"She'd followed us that day, and when she saw us together she flew into a rage. She attacked with a spell, aiming for our clasped hands. But her heart was full of hate, and only dark magic answered. The spell turned on her, and she was left with two gnarled claws instead of hands."

Isabel's mouth hung open. "What happened then?"

"She screamed and cursed and swore I'd pay for breaking my word, even if it took her the rest of her life." Caelia sighed. "Then she flew from the Wood, headed west toward the mountains."

"And?" Fiona asked.

"We never saw her again," Caelia said. "But it must be her that you saw."

"It does make sense," Manzy said.

"The elder who shines tonight sensed dark magic from that direction," Caelia said, shaking her head. "I should've known it was Annis. But it's been so long, so many years. I thought that...that maybe she'd forgiven me."

"Forgiven you?" Fiona asked, huffing. "She sounds crazier than an eight-legged dog."

"But now she has a Sarastro. And Jaydin and you," Caelia said, looking at Fiona, her eyes swelling with tears, "and that poor boy, have paid the price. I should've seen this coming. I should've been more prepared."

"But Caelia," Fiona said, wrinkling her brow, "the old woman I saw didn't look like a fairy."

"Which is why we were confused by the Sarastro," Manzy added.

"She didn't even have wings," Fiona continued, "and she was coated in ice. Maybe it isn't Annis after all."

"But child," Caelia said, wiping her eyes, "it's hard to ignore the claws." She sighed. "Only the Angels know what has become of her, all this time with nothing but bitterness to keep her company."

Fiona nodded, knowing all too well how it felt to be alone, to feel like your whole world had disappeared. She reached to her neck and unconsciously rubbed the old key between her fingers.

"How does Graven figure into any of this?" Rhiannon asked.

"Bright Eye operatives have been surveilling Graven for some time," Kevin said. "He is simply doing what he does best. Taking advantage. He may be targeting the King, but as far as we can discern, you lot fell into his lap, just like Jaydin and the Neulock boy."

The room was silent, except for the sound of Cricket bouncing back and forth on an enchanted toadstool.

"Well, it's not over yet," Fiona said, weighing her options. She could only think of two. Head east to the castle, counting on the King's good nature and mercy. Or continue west for the mountains and find Annis.

Both were awful. Convincing the King would be difficult, even with Caelia backing her up. He'd likely dismiss the Queen as a fearful mother, eager to tell any story that would stop her son's execution. And Fiona already knew how he felt about her.

Going in search of Annis was equally troubling. No one knew where in the vast Bitter Mountains she lived, or if she was even there at all. And supposing she was lucky enough to find the old hag, what then? Blow through the door and ask her to take it all back? She was a dangerous, vindictive fairy who'd been nursing a grudge for fifteen years. And she had a Sarastro.

To make matters worse, Fiona knew with every labored breath and each small tickle in her throat that her time was running out. In less than two days her debt would be paid, one way or another.

17

Shine On

KNOCK! KNOCK!

Caelia's eyes flicked to the door.

KNOCK! KNOCK!

Manzy trotted over, pinched the handle in her teeth, and opened the door, but no one was there. She leaned her head into the dark forest, but still found nothing.

"You again?" came a tiny voice from above.

Manzy looked up and saw the dragonfly fairy from the Moonshadow, hovering above her head. "Feeling better?" she asked smartly as she backed into the Hollow.

"Hmmph," he said, and zipped past her, buzzing through the air almost too fast to be seen. He stopped in front of his Queen. "My lady," he chimed, "the old one says it is time." He dashed around in excited circles, sending the lightning bugs into a frenzy. They scattered, clouding the air with a frantic, blinking flurry.

Caelia cupped her hand below her mouth and whispered so softly it was nothing but a purr. The glow bugs returned to the walls, calm as before. "I'm afraid I must go," she said, floating toward the door. "But please, join us. You're unlikely to see this again in your lifetime." She swept into the forest, followed by the little dragonfly fairy.

"Come on," Fiona said, heading to the door, "you heard Caelia."

"But, shouldn't we...," Manzy protested.

"Shouldn't we what? I'm not missing an elder's Shine," Fiona said over her shoulder, already feeling her throat getting scratchy. "Besides, how long could it take?"

Manzy huffed, but followed. Cricket and Isabel rode along on Manzy's back, while Rhiannon walked with Kevin, telling him about the day before in the tunnels.

Outside the grand party was in full swing. The sounds from across the Wood were raucous; voices shouting, mixed with what had to be the entire Wood clapping in unison. And over it all was the thunder of uproarious cheering, accented by great bursts of laughter.

They followed the growing sounds, which now included a garbled, bawdy song about Foster in his younger days. Isabel grinned from ear to ear and tapped Manzy's neck to the rhythm as she rode. Cricket was so excited she stood on her feet, bouncing up and down and looking over Manzy's head, trying to see what was going on.

The moon was full, casting a glossy luminescence onto their path. Fiona noticed how the pearly light made Manzy's hide nearly sparkle. It was so beautiful she closed her eyes and vowed to enjoy this moment, to forget for awhile how desperate things had become.

Their path led them through the forest, to a massive gathering surrounding the Rowan Oak. As they squirmed through the crowd of hovering fairies and woodland creatures, inching forward to get a better view, they heard Caelia's voice above the clamor. She hovered in front of the tree's flowing, peacock branches.

"Thank you all," she began. She opened her wide, purple wings and floated into the sky. All eyes were drawn to her unmistakable beauty and power.

Fiona found herself up front, beside Rhiannon. Kevin was curled on the ground, poking his head up so he could see. Fiona knelt down and offered him her arm.

"Thank you," he said, and coiled up behind her neck, where he settled comfortably on her shoulders.

Manzy and the young girls were up front too. The fairies floated around them, making room to share this spectacular event. Some even joined Isabel and Cricket, settling their delicate little bodies on Manzy.

"Tonight we witness a great fairy at his best," Caelia continued, "an old one in his final bit of magic." She smirked and lowered herself a bit. The crowd cheered loudly, their beating wings creating a small breeze in the summer air.

Caelia raised her hands and the crowd calmed. She floated down farther, hovering just above them, and shook her crown of golden hair until it cascaded over her shoulders. Her lavender eyes sparkled in the moonlight, entreating them to rejoice.

"Tonight, my sweet ones," she said, sweeping her long arms to the sides, "is Foster's glorious time of Shine!"

The fairies erupted in applause and whooping shouts, and this time she made no effort to calm them. This time she gave them Foster.

He flew from the crowd at the mention of his name. He was almost invisible; nothing but a pale shadow of what he'd once been. Had it not been for the smoldering pipe in his hand, he would've been nearly impossible to see.

"Hey there, Foster!" a rowdy voice called out, "are you a fairy or a flickerfawn? I can't see a thing besides that bouncing pipe of yours!"

"Aye, and be glad of it!" he responded, his broad grin hidden from view, "for right now I am offering you my full share of the moon!"

The crowd cheered at his jest, then waited, eager for whatever the grand old fairy would say next.

The pipe danced in the air as he brought it to his mouth. He drew on it until the embers glowed bright orange. A puff of smoke appeared as the faint figure exhaled, and he began again.

"My time is here, as well you know.
And to the Mother, I gladly go.
My bones are old, my skin is bare,
I leave now without a care.

~ 115 ~

"But 'ere I do, I've a 'piece to say.
For one we miss on this happy day.
Of Jaydin I speak! Our Guardian lad!"

The crowd had been laughing with Foster as he spoke, but now, at the mention of the Queen's imprisoned son, a hush fell over them.

Foster smiled, pleased with this last bit of mischief. He flipped in the air, sending the feathery branches of the Oak waving as he tumbled in a few somersaults. His pipe twirled before them, a burning ember suspended in the air.

"Held so long for something bad," he continued, hovering in front of Fiona. She could just make out the faint outline of his wrinkled face. His fading blue eyes twinkled.

"Twas her that done it, with magic black.
I felt it, I did! Crawling up my back," and he winked at Fiona.

The outline of Foster's body began to glow. It spread until he became a brilliant figure of shining white, hovering before them. Fiona held her hand to her eyes, and Kevin hid under her collar.

"Three times as high and onward go,
Through wretched cold and blinding snow.

Foster's brightly glowing body started to give off heat. It radiated across the gathering, sending waves of warmth through the crowd. He laughed, one final time, then said,

"And where winds blow o'er stony crags
Inside she be....the wretched hag!"

Before the last word was barely free of his lips, he rolled into a large ball and grew impossibly bright, painful to those who didn't look away. He floated slowly, higher into the air, a shining star amongst them in the Wood. And with an ear splitting BOOM! the ball of light exploded into a dazzling shower of colorful sparks. They rained on the cheering crowd, a spectacular display of radiance, sparkling in the night as the old fairy was finally one with his Mother. No one even noticed when his pipe fell from the sky, landing on the forest floor with a soft thud.

18

Powers

"Fiona, you can't," Caelia said. Her wings fluttered behind her as she paced the Hollow. "It's too dangerous. I will go again and plead for Jaydin. A thousand times if need!"

"What about Fiona?" Manzy shouted. The girl was sitting on the floor, still recovering from the latest coughing spell that had come after arguing with Caelia. "What about the debt?"

"I don't know!" Caelia shouted. She stopped and took a deep breath. "I don't know," she repeated, more calmly. "But there is nothing Fiona could do in the mountains. There is nothing she could do against Annis. And going in search of her is madness. It's suicide."

Fiona laughed and crawled to her feet. "Come on," she said, looking at their grim faces, "that's kind of funny, don't you think? A suicide mission, when I'm already, you know?"

She walked to Caelia, shaking her head. "I'm going to the mountains. And after what Foster said, I might even find her." She shrugged her shoulders, knowing the whole thing was pretty unlikely.

Caelia opened her mouth to protest, but Fiona cut her off. "Besides," she said, smiling, "what's she going to do, kill me?"

Fiona knew she'd be lucky to even make it to the mountains. It was a two day ride just to the foothills, assuming Manzy would even agree to go, and hard climbing through snow covered mountains after that. The whole thing was impossible. But she had to try.

"Miss Caelia," Isabel asked quietly, "is Brent going to die?"

Caelia sighed. "I don't know, child. The Carapacem Spell is awful, dark magic. It paralyzes, giving the appearance of death while the victim remains aware. Aware of the thirst that scratches their throat and the stabbing hunger that gnaws at their belly. It is more cruel than any magic I've seen in my long years."

"One more reason to go," Fiona said, looking around the room. She saw nothing but leaden, depressed looks.

She clapped her hands together and jumped on the stone table. The effort cost her and she began to wheeze. "This witch comes between Caelia and Lindley," she said, catching her breath, "then uses Jaydin to curse an innocent little boy and you're all going to let her get away with it?" She looked at them, daring them to disagree. "Well, I'm not." She jumped down. "I'm going."

The princesses sat, eyes wide as saucers watching Fiona. Kevin sat with Cricket, silent as well. Only Manzy looked away. She knew it was foolish to argue with Fiona once she'd made up her mind. Caelia would no more be able to stop her from searching for Annis than Foster could've prevented his own Shine.

Caelia walked to Fiona. She gazed into the girl's eyes. "We are lucky to call you friend. If you are sure, I would not stand in your way."

"Thank you," Fiona said, bowing slightly. "Can you take the girls back with you tomorrow?"

"WHAT?" Rhiannon shouted. "We're not going anywhere near the castle. Graven is waiting for us. Besides, the longer he's searching for us, the longer he's not killing Father." She huffed and shook her head. "We're going with you."

"No, you're not. It's too dangerous. You heard Caelia," Fiona said, waving her arms in the air, "ancient evil magic. Just hide out or something until you see Ferront. You can trust him, right?" She turned to Caelia. "Or take them back to Dee & Mickey's."

"Fiona," Rhiannon said, "I'm just as stubborn as you."

Isabel nodded her head. "Yeah, she really is."

"Perhaps it would be best if you travelled with me," Caelia said. "I could see you safely to your father, and you could explain about the mistaken kidnapping. Please, I insist."

"No, thank you," Rhiannon said, holding her head high. She cleared her throat. "We're going with Fiona. She needs us."

"Well that's just not true," Fiona said. She looked at Caelia. "We could spend the rest of my life arguing with her. Trust me." She turned back to Rhiannon. "It's your funeral. Don't say I didn't warn you."

Caelia settled lightly in her chair. She brought her hands together and pressed the tips of her fingers to her silvery lips. "Since you've all decided to put yourselves in mortal peril, the least I can do is offer some assistance."

"I'm already in mortal peril," Fiona said, smiling.

Manzy bumped her with her head. "Knock it off. It's not funny."

"What do you mean, Miss Caelia?" Isabel asked.

"Nothing really," she said with a smile. "Just a few gifts I'd like to bestow upon you young warriors."

She leaned forward and called to Fiona. At Caelia's urging, the girl knelt before her on the mossy floor.

"In an effort to help you rise above the filth that you so willingly trudge through," she said with a wink, "to you, Fiona Thorn, constant friend of the Wood, I bestow the gift of Levitation."

Fiona's eyes widened. She'd known Caelia was capable of all kinds of magic, and was especially skilled at healing, but never in all the years she'd known her had Caelia even hinted she could share any of her magic.

Caelia cupped her hand under her mouth and whispered, "*Aeronatare...Aeronatare.*" Her palm began to sparkle as the spell awakened. She met Fiona's nervous glance and blew into her palm, sending the glittering air of enchantment into Fiona's face.

"Now say '*Assurgam*'," Caelia instructed.

Fiona raised her eyebrows and did as she was told.

Everyone watched in astonishment as Fiona began to rise from the mossy floor of the Hollow, floating into the air above them, her knees still tucked under her. "Caelia," Fiona asked shakily as she watched the ground growing farther and farther away, "is this supposed to be happening?"

"Of course," she answered, "you are levitating."

Fiona looked down at her body and realized that her legs were still bent, as if she were sitting on her knees. She nervously stretched her legs until she was upright. She was floating higher and higher up in the hollow of the tree. "Can I come down now?"

"If you want to come down," Caelia said, "then do so. It is your power now. Concentrate. Control it."

Fiona stiffened her body and began to sink, then quickly rose through the air again, losing any progress she'd made. Her face twisted in concentration as she floated up and down, like a human yo-yo, trying to master her gift.

"Princess Isabel," Caelia said, "come forward, please. We may as well have you all learning at the same time."

Isabel hopped in front of Caelia, still watching Fiona.

"Princess," Caelia said, and Isabel turned to her.

"Sorry, Miss Caelia, but I've never seen anyone fly before. It's my most favorite thing."

"But child, that's not flying. This is flying. To you, who has wished so long for the sky, I give the Wings of Sebelia." She cupped her hand before her mouth and whispered, "*Glissadia Ascenti...Glissadia Ascenti.*"

As before, the air in her palm began to sparkle with power. She looked into Isabel's unbelieving face and blew gently, sending her the power to fly.

"Oh thank you so much!" Isabel said, bouncing around in front of her. "Thank you! Thank you! Thank you!"

"Well are you going to fly or what?" Rhiannon asked, laughing.

"How does it work, Miss Caelia? How?"

"To take flight, you must say, 'Volo'."

Isabel held her arms to the side, squeezed her eyes shut and whispered.

The room was filled with gasps and murmurs of wonderment as flame red feathers began to sprout from under Isabel's outstretched arms. They continued to grow, reaching down and curving back toward her body, where they attached themselves to her hip. Isabel looked down at her new accessories. "That didn't even hurt!" She spun around and looked at everyone. "Look you guys! I've got wings! Pretty red ones!"

"Fantastic!" Manzy shouted, rearing up on her hind legs.

"Izzy! Izzy!" Cricket cried, flapping her arms as she ran around in circles.

"That is positively the most extraordinarily astonishing occurrence I have ever had the pleasure to witness!" Kevin said.

"Huh?"

"He thinks it's cool!" Fiona shouted from above. "Come on, give 'em a try!"

"So fly already!" Rhiannon said, waving her arms above her head. "What are you waiting for?"

"It's just that," Isabel said, hanging her head, "I've always wanted to fly. But even with wings, I still don't know how."

"Princess," Caelia said firmly, "believe that you can fly. The magic will do the rest."

Isabel nodded. She moved her arms up and down, slowly at first, then more rapidly. They could feel the air moving through the room, rushing past them as her feathery red wings beat faster and faster. Isabel closed her eyes and whispered, "Volo," and slowly, her feet lifted off the ground. She instinctively leaned forward and to everyone's surprise, began to glide effortlessly through the air.

"I'M FLYING! I'M FLYING!"

She expertly circled around Fiona, who was still trying to master her levitation, then boldly dove toward the ground like a hawk on the hunt.

"THAT was AWESOME!" she said as she landed precisely in front of Rhiannon.

"You're well suited to flight, " Caelia said, nodding in approval. "When you are finished flying, your wings will disappear. But you need only whisper, and they will sprout once again."

"Thank you so much!" Isabel said as Cricket came running over to touch her feathers.

"Princess Rhiannon," Caelia said, "would you like your gift?"

"Very much, ma'am." She knelt before the queen in her chair.

"For you, a different gift," Caelia said, her lilting words easing Rhiannon's anxiety. "You have longed to speak to other creatures, have you not?"

Rhiannon nodded eagerly.

"For you, Princess Rhiannon, I offer the Iomlan Tongue." She looked down into Rhiannon's confused face and smiled. "The gift of speaking to animals."

She raised her palm and said, *"Scriptum Varmintia...Scriptum Varmintia"* until the dancing sparks appeared. She blew gently and sent Rhiannon's gift whispering through the air. The glowing lights hovered between them, then circled Rhiannon's head before disappearing.

Nothing seemed to change. She looked questioningly at Caelia. The Fairy Queen raised her eyebrows and gestured for Rhiannon to join the others.

"Thank you," the princess said, trying to hide her disappointment. She sat down beside Kevin as Caelia called to Cricket.

Cricket hopped around up front as the others watched. Isabel was resting beside Manzy, catching her breath after so much flying. She was proudly showing her feathers to Fiona, who had finally figured out how to control her levitation and had even managed to land softly on Manzy's back.

"What gift for you, little warrior?" Caelia said, watching Cricket carefully.

"You should give her flame hands or something," Fiona suggested, catching her breath.

"Very funny, Fee," Manzy said. "We'd do nothing but put out fires all day."

"I wasn't kidding. She can handle it. Just look at her! She's a fierce little warrior!"

Cricket was bent over in front of Caelia, with her bottom facing the rest of them. She had her head resting on the mossy floor and was trying to spin around in a circle.

"I don't think she'd do that, Kevin," Rhiannon said, pursing her lips.

But Kevin hadn't said anything.

"I doubt it as well, Princess. I just wouldn't want...HEY!" He whipped his head toward Rhiannon. "I didn't say that out loud."

Rhiannon's face lit up as she realized she'd heard his thoughts. It thrilled her more than she'd imagined.

"Miss Caelia," Isabel called, "what about wings for her too? I bet she'd like to fly. Can you make hers purple? It's her favorite color."

Cricket started flapping her arms up and down again, laughing.

"I believe," Caelia said, gazing at Cricket, "something to even the odds."

Her words had drawn Cricket's attention, and the little princess watched with wide, trusting eyes as Caelia brought her cupped palm to her lips and whispered, "*Aspector Amendium...Aspector Amendium.*"

"What is it, Miss Caelia?" Isabel asked after the sparkling light had faded.

Caelia held her finger to the others, urging patience, and called Cricket into her lap, explaining in low whispers how to work the new power.

Cricket listened patiently, then nodded. She hopped from Caelia's lap and pointed at Kevin, her eyes lit with pure joy, and shouted, "BIG!"

Kevin's body began to quiver. His coils shook and his dark scales vibrated as he blew up to a hundred times his normal size. His body towered above them, reaching way up into the tree, a giant mass of coiled, glittering snake. His wide, black and yellow eyes flashed above, each of his long lashes now the size of a small tree branch.

The girls scrambled to the other side of the room, trying to find somewhere in the suddenly cramped Hollow that wasn't pressed with snake coils.

. "AKE! AKE!"

"Cricket," Rhiannon said seriously, "he doesn't like this. Put him back."

"Yes please, Princess!" Kevin shouted from high above. "I, I, oh no..."

"DUCK!" Rhiannon shouted.

"ACHOO!"

The Hollow reverberated with the sneeze. Great gobs of snake snot drizzled through the air, soaking everything below. The frightened lightning bugs took flight immediately, buzzing through the snotty mist.

Caelia wiped her face and whispered softly to Cricket.

"Hurry up, Cricket!" Rhiannon said. "He's gonna' do it again!"

Cricket laughed and pointed a chubby finger at Kevin. "MALL! MALL!"

They all watched, waiting expectantly. But nothing happened.

"Princess, please," Kevin said, "This size is not...ACHOO!...conducive to espionage."

Another storm of snake snot rained over them, soaking into their gowns and drenching their hair

Caelia held Cricket's hand and helped. The little girl pointed again at her best friend and shouted, "MALL! SM..SMALL!"

Kevin began to shake. Thousands of lightning bugs fluttered through the damp air as his giant coiled body rumbled with the spell. And then, he was gone.

Well, not really. He was back to normal, laying amidst the crumbled ruins of the stone table. But he looked so small now, compared to the giant he'd just been, that it was almost like he was gone.

"Are you okay?" Isabel asked as they all skidded in front of him, swatting at the few scattered bugs in the air.

"He's fine," Rhiannon said, before he had a chance to answer.

Kevin looked at her and winced. "How long will this continue?"

"You must learn to block her," Caelia said, "and you, Princess, must learn to be patient. Not everything you hear needs to be shared."

Cricket ran over and began playing with Kevin's tail. Her eyes glittered and she looked around. She lifted her hand, pointed her finger at Manzy and...

"NO!" everyone shouted. Isabel quickly opened her wings and blocked her little sister's dangerous finger.

Caelia scooped Cricket up and flew behind the fern screen. The others could hear nothing but hushed whispers as Caelia tried, once again, to teach Cricket to control her power.

"Close one, huh, Manz?" Fiona said, "Told you. Flame hands would've been better."

"I'm afraid I'd be nothing but cinders had that been her gift," Kevin said, shaking his head.

Caelia emerged from the screen, smiling. Cricket tottled along beside her.

"I am sorry. I did not anticipate that. I have given her the power of Enlargement. And its twin, Compression. But I have helped her, and all of you," she said, wincing as she wiped her arms clean of snake snot, "with her gift."

She looked down fondly at Cricket. "From now on, she will need permission from one of you before her power will work. It is a common binding spell, used mainly for small ones." She smiled at Kevin. "I am truly sorry. It won't happen again."

"What are you apologizing to him for?" Fiona asked, squeezing her boogie soaked, slimy hair, "we're the ones that got the worst of it."

19

Wildlife

"Look out below!" Fiona called. She dropped the wood to the ground, laughing when it bounced behind Manzy, causing her to jump. "I warned you," she hollered, then swore under her breath as another coughing fit erupted. They'd been coming more often, especially when she forgot to keep her voice down.

She was hovering near the top of a tall pine tree, scavenging for dead branches. A tree this size was a rare find in the rocky terrain of the lower mountains and Fiona meant to take advantage of it. The dry wood would make an excellent fire.

Once she and Manzy had gathered a bit more they could rejoin the others at the campsite. They'd had to wander more than a mile, but tonight when they sat before a roaring fire, it would be worth it. She was looking forward to a restful night under the stars. She was more tired than she'd been in awhile.

Isabel had done well as a scout. She'd spotted a small, flat area of rock, surrounded by giant boulders on three sides that butted up against a steeper part of the mountain. The stone had been warm from baking in the sun all day, and would shelter them as the night grew colder. It wasn't ideal, but with the help of a fire, it would work.

The group had left Caelia and the Wood behind early that morning, traveling northeast, across the Winding River into the Bitter Mountains. They'd made good time, covering more distance in one day than any of them had expected. Fiona had quickly discovered that she could move twice as fast if she hovered, and Isabel's feet had barely touched the ground since they left. She preferred gliding through the warm air, scouting the path ahead.

Rhiannon and Manzy had traveled quickly as well, taking advantage of an old cart path that wound through the base of the mountain. With Kevin racing swiftly beside them, the three worked together on honing Rhiannon's ability to discern the thoughts of one woodland creature from another, and on both of them being able to block her when they wanted more privacy.

They'd made astonishing progress. Rhiannon had learned the difference between the frenzied thoughts of a nesting bluebird and the ravenous hunger that came from predators. Like the fox that'd been hiding in the brush late that morning. Rhiannon had spent a tense minute as it considered how long it could survive on a kill the size of Cricket. It was tempted, wondering how to get the plump little one away from the group, but finally decided it wasn't worth the risk. Rhiannon had smiled, knowing she'd influenced the fox by sending a resounding "NO!" into its confused head.

For Cricket, the day had been magical. She hadn't been allowed to use her power, but she'd been able to fly with her sister. She clung to Isabel's back, screeching with delight as they twisted and dove through the air, gliding and climbing as they explored the sky. And when she inevitably grew tired of flying, she rode with Rhiannon, tempting hungry foxes into battles they couldn't begin to imagine.

The day had been warm and bright, with an ocean of clear blue sky overhead. The air was filled with laughter and a thrilling sense of adventure as they perfected their exciting new powers and explored the beautiful countryside. And while the snow covered peaks of the Bitter Mountains loomed, their icy crags rising in the distance with the promise of darker, unknown dangers, they were distant. And for now, out of mind.

"Come on, Fee," Manzy called from the base of the tree, "I think we've got enough!"

"You sure?" Fiona answered, careful not to shout. "I bet I could find some more!"

"I'm sure I've had enough of wood dropping from above my head." She stretched, trying to see Fiona. But she'd lost her in the glare of the setting sun.

"Fiona!" she called. "Come on! It's almost dark."

Manzy shook her body, sending an orangish cloud of dust flying. She lazily scanned the ground for anything to munch on while she waited. She was rewarded with a small patch of oniongrass growing in the shade of the tree. She stepped forward, already tasting the spicy greens, and heard something behind her. Her head jerked up and her ears tipped back, listening.

"Fiona, is that you?" she asked, slowly turning around.

"I'm coming! I'm coming!" the girl said from above.

Not Fiona, Manzy thought, *she's still messing around in the tree.*

Her body grew tense, every muscle on alert as she eased toward the shadowy boulders where the noise had come from. The light wind blowing down the mountain was making it difficult to smell anything. She rubbed her muzzle across the top of the warm rock, searching for a scent, and got more than she'd bargained for. Her head shot up and her body tingled with fear.

"FIONA!"

Manzy spun around and saw nothing but claws streaking toward her. She ducked just in time; a mouth full of pointed teeth flew by her head as the cat landed on her back. It scrambled toward the base of her tail and sunk its claws in, hissing as it fought to stay on.

"FIONA!" Manzy shrieked. She bucked and twisted, struggling to lose the howling Spotted Cat from her back. But it was too late. The cat had gotten the advantage; down low, lying flat and gripping with its razor sharp claws.

The cat raised its head, distracted by movement in the air.

"I'M COMING!" Fiona screamed as she dropped from the tree, heading for her pack. She dug furiously, ignoring the drops of blood that sprayed on her bag as she coughed. She grabbed the Hazard Bow and swung around, aiming at the cat. It was impossible to get a clean shot; Manzy was bucking wildly, and if she missed she'd hit her.

She glided closer, her heart pounding as she fought to catch her breath and get a better shot. The cat howled as Fiona closed in. Fresh streams of bright red ran over Manzy's hide. The cat dug deeper with its claws, gripping its struggling prize, trying to hang on. It bared its fangs and hissed at Fiona. She hovered around the battling pair, kicking out with her feet and watching for the right moment to take her shot.

It glared at her, challenging her with hatred in its green eyes, and buried its teeth into Manzy's bucking rear.

"AHHHH!!!"

Fiona raised her bow.

Now or never. That cat is tearing her apart.

She aimed carefully. Her finger gently gripped the trigger. She said a silent prayer to the Angels and...

She was knocked sideways, flung through the air by what felt a flying hippo.

It's payback, a crazy corner of her mind shouted, for blasting them out of their watering hole.

She slammed into the boulders, the wind knocked completely out of her.

This is what's coming if I don't pay the debt.

She hit so hard that even as she fought for the breath that wouldn't come, even as she struggled for air to fill her empty, burning lungs, she knew her shoulder was broken.

She slid down the warm rock, feeling nothing but searing pain above her left arm. Then her shoulder was skipping painfully over the ground as the large male cat drug her by her boot, away from the boulders. He pinned her against the rocky ground with both front claws, holding her down with more strength than she would've thought possible for a body half her size.

STUPID! Why wasn't I looking for the mate?

She opened her eyes and screamed, writhing and squirming on the ground as she kicked and tried desperately to escape the deadly cat. It growled and hissed as she rolled from side to side, squeezing its claws deep into left her arm and the side of her neck. She felt a blinding heat burn her neck as the sharp

~ 129 ~

nails pierced her flesh. And then, a slippery warmth sliding down her skin and soaking into her tunic that could only be her own blood.

She thrashed her arms and ripped at the heavy, furry body that held her to the ground. But she couldn't make it move. It was just too strong.

She fought hard, squirming underneath, coughing and trying to catch her breath, while the cat held her down and waited. For while she didn't know it, she was losing so much blood that the Spotted Cat could almost taste it on the air.

He sat atop her chest, hissing with his ears pressed flat against his head, pinning her to the ground in what was beginning to look like the fight of her life.

But it wasn't a bloody death Fiona saw in these last moments. It was Manzy.

She rolled her head to the side and saw her life's match. The horse had backed herself up against the large wall of boulders and had reared up on her hind legs. She was slamming the female cat, still clinging to her hind end, over and over into the rocks. The struggling cat finally let go, screaming in frustration as it scampered up the rocks and began pacing back and forth. It shook its dizzy head and watched its prey go free.

Manzy limped toward Fiona, ignoring her own gushing wound, and briefly, their eyes met. Manzy's flashed wide and white with fear as she stalked a circle around Fiona and the cat. Fiona was lying on her back in a growing pool of her own blood, trapped by the male of the mated pair. She was still conscious, but barely.

"Fight Fiona! Don't give up on me!"

Manzy struck out with her front hoofs, and the cat licked his lips, daring her to come closer. His wiry whiskers twitched in anticipation of the kill.

Fiona saw Manzy and smiled weakly. At least she'd gotten free. That was what mattered now. She was too tired to worry about anything else. She couldn't even remember why they were here anyway. Manzy would know. She could finish it, whatever it was.

Fiona felt herself drifting from the pain, giving in to the weight on her chest, giving in to the darkness. Dying wasn't so bad. At least she'd finally get to meet her parents. She reached for her necklace, but the effort was too much.

"FIONA!"

Manzy's desperate cry shook her and her eyes opened.

Fight. Don't give up.

She reached toward the cat's head with her hands, though they'd never felt so heavy in her life, and wrapped her fingers around its thick neck. Her arms went numb, stinging and tingling, as she gripped with the last of her failing strength. She squeezed until there was nothing left to give, until her arms gave out and fell limply to the side.

It wasn't enough. But Manzy could still get away, she thought as she began to black out again.

Run Manzy! Run!

The great weight of the cat slumped forward, collapsing onto her. It held her down, choking her in its fur. The dead cat was pressing against her face, making it impossible to breathe.

Just my luck to choke the thing and now suffocate under it.

But then it was moving, sliding slowly over her face, filling her mouth with disgusting fur as it stuck to her tongue. She gasped for breath, coughed and winced as the air filled her lungs, reminding her body of how broken it was.

She slowly opened her eyes, expecting to find Manzy. Instead, she saw two dark figures standing over her. One of them was holding a bloody arrow. They were talking, mumbling something she couldn't understand.

She squinted at them, and rolled her head to the side, trying to see who they were. But their faces were dark, obscured by the shadows as the sun set swiftly behind them. She was drifting again, floating in a sea of black. Her eyes were heavy and she needed to sleep. She could rest for a little while, she thought, now that the danger had passed.

She looked hard, one last time, trying to see something she could recognize. And then, to her horror, she did.

Flickering above them, in the chilly mountain wind, she saw a black vulture gripping a frog in its mighty talons. She opened her mouth to scream, but the breath stuck in her throat, making nothing but a soft gagging sound. And then she was sinking, falling headfirst into the surrounding darkness.

The campsite was very cozy. Just like a house, but out in nature. It had three big boulders for walls, set up against the mountain, and a nice flat floor. And as long as it didn't rain, which never happened in the summer, they didn't need a roof. Isabel stood back, her wings collapsed, her hands on her hips, and admired their handiwork.

She and her sisters had spent the last hour collecting little bits of grasses and whatever soft shrubbery they could find. It hadn't been as hard as they'd thought. There was life all over the dry mountainside if you looked. Before long, the three of them had a big enough pile of grasses to make four small pillows.

"See," Isabel said proudly, "I told you we could do it."

Rhiannon nodded. "Yes, you did. Now can I stop hearing about it?"

Isabel shrugged her shoulders. She smiled and reached for Cricket, who was bouncing up and down in the big pile of grasses.

Kevin opened his eyes as the little girl squealed with delight, then went back to his nap. He'd also been lucky that evening, finding an abandoned nest of hawk eggs at the top of a tall rock. Now he was very full, still loaded down with half of the large rat from the Wood, plus the eggs. He wanted nothing more than to spend the rest of the night coiled in the corner against the soothingly warm rock and sleep.

"It's getting dark, Rhi. I'm hungry. When do you think they'll be back?" Isabel asked as she caught her breath. She'd been chasing Cricket around the campsite, making the little girl laugh loudly.

"I don't know," Rhiannon answered, "but settle down." She looked seriously at the two of them. "You don't know what's out there. Be quiet. Besides," she said smiling at Kevin, "you're bothering the snake."

"Perhaps your sister is right," Kevin said sleepily, ignoring Rhiannon's announcement of his thoughts. "Excessive levels of hilarity are," and he yawned, fluttering his eyelashes a few times, "most assuredly for the daylight hours."

"AKE! AKE!" Cricket shouted as she bounced his way, "PLAY AKE! PLAY!"

"Oh child," he began, but was interrupted by a rumbling behind one of the boulders. The sound of crunching rock was everywhere, bouncing through the campsite, surrounding them as one of the back walls began to rock from side to side.

"Isabel, take her and go!" Rhiannon shouted, reaching for her Hazard Bow. She sensed what was behind the boulder, pushing it forward. She stood in the corner with her finger on the trigger.

"What? What is it?" Isabel asked as she grabbed Cricket.

"Just go!"

Isabel took off with Cricket clinging to her back. They flew into the coming darkness. As they circled back around, Isabel squinted, not believing what she saw.

A monstrous creature was behind the boulder. It was hunched over, pushing the small mountain of rock, but was still taller than her father or any man she'd ever seen.

But this creature was no man. It was an ogre.

She and Cricket buzzed above the ruined campsite, watching in horror. The ogre's leathery brown hide rippled with muscle. It wore a pair of dirty trousers, frayed and ripped at the knees. Its arms were thick and ended in three-fingered hands that pressed flat against the large boulder, pushing it out of the way.

Isabel was mesmerized, watching as a creature from her imagination, from her Uncle Ferront's tales, came to life before her eyes. It leaned forward, pressing its huge shoulder into the rock and heaved forward.

"AHRRRGGGRAAHH!"

A thunderous growl shook the air, and as the ogre finally shoved the giant boulder out of its way, Isabel woke to the very real danger they were in. She shook her head and dove toward Rhiannon.

She found her big sister struggling to reload her bow. The first arrow had exploded in a blazing fury, sending glass and debris shooting throughout the campsite. What it hadn't done was even nick the hide of the ogre. He lumbered slowly toward Rhiannon.

"It's not working!" Isabel shouted. "Climb up!"

Rhiannon shook her head. "Hang on!" If she could tell Fiona she'd bested a mountain ogre the girl would have no choice but to give her some respect.

But when the second exploding arrow bounced off the ogre's waist, doing nothing but singeing his pants, Rhiannon decided her sister was right. She ran to the boulder behind her and started climbing out of the campsite.

Kevin hid below, coiled in the corner, hissing menacingly.

"It's an ogre!" Isabel shouted from above, her eyes darting to the beast. It shuffled toward them, rumbling deep under its breath.

"*You think?*" Rhiannon said as she fought to keep her legs from getting tangled in her dress.

"Geez, Rhi," Isabel whined, "you don't have to be so mean."

"He's hungry," Rhiannon said, her frightened eyes meeting her sister's. "I can tell. He's really hungry."

"Give me your hand!" Isabel said, reaching down.

"You can't hold me! You're not strong enough!" Rhiannon shouted.

"I can! Trust me!"

Rhiannon clasped her left hand around Isabel's wrist and held on as hard as she could.

"AKE!" Cricket cried from Isabel's back. Then she dove headfirst for Kevin.

Isabel twisted in the air, thrown off balance by Cricket.

"Cricket! Sit still!" she yelled, trying to keep a grip on Rhiannon's hand. "We have to help Rhi!"

Cricket made a face, but sat up.

Rhiannon scrambled her feet against the rock as she dangled from Isabel, struggling to climb out of the campsite. But she was dirty and sweaty and her mind was filled with the ogre's rumbling hunger, filled with thoughts of how her bones would crunch like a big chicken. She felt the back of her throat close, making it hard to breathe, and her hand began to slip.

"Hold on!" Isabel shouted. "Don't fall!"

"FOOO!" the ogre bellowed, angry his food was getting away.

Rhiannon looked behind her. He was within arm's reach now, and when she saw his face she screamed.

He had a heap of scrunched up skin for a nose and his eyes were sunken so deep in the folds of skin they were nothing but dark, wet pin pricks.

But it was his mouth, full of ugly teeth, that had made her scream. There were two long ones at each end, like elephant tusks, and four others in between, all blunted and worn. Perfect for crunching bones.

"Rhi!" Isabel screamed, trying to hold Rhiannon's hand as it slipped away. "Hold on! You have to hold on!"

Rhiannon reached with her other hand and clamped onto Isabel. "GO! GO!" she shouted.

"FOOO!" the ogre growled, closer now.

Isabel took off, beating her powerful wings, but she felt resistance. She was sinking, slowing being dragged out of the sky.

"Izzy!" Rhiannon screamed. "He's got me!"

The ogre had Rhiannon by the thigh, his three fingered hand closed around her leg like a drumstick.

Rhiannon looked up at her sisters, her eyes full of fear, and let go, freeing them from the hungry ogre.

"Rhi!" Isabel cried from above.

The ogre plucked Rhiannon from the side of the boulder and dangled her in front of his face. His tusks danced on his jaw and his thoughts flooded her mind like a raging river, making it hard to think of anything other than how good she was going to taste.

Rhiannon shook her head, trying to block him from her mind, but he was so big and so hungry. She dangled upside down in his tight grip, swinging back and forth, trying to break free. She kicked and pounded on his arm, but it was no use; it was like punching a tree.

The ogre shuffled toward the cave.

"HELP!! HELP!! He's going to eat me!!" she screamed as the ogre swung her through the air, batting at something around his head.

It was Isabel, swooping at the ogre like a buzzing mosquito.

"IZZZZZYYYYYYYY! This isn't HELLPIINGG!"

Isabel dove toward the ground, circling for another attack and saw Kevin. He was hanging from the ogre's foot, his fangs sunk in the giant big toe. The ogre's thick toenail curved out in front, and Kevin was curled around it, his teeth stuck in the beast's rough hide.

"What are you doing?" Isabel asked as she flew by.

"I'm...UCK!" he cried through a mouthful of ogre toe.

"Mall, Izzy! Mall?" Cricket begged from Isabel's back as they climbed toward the ogre's head.

"Yes, Cricket! Yes! Make him small!" Isabel said. "That's a great idea!"

The ogre turned his head back and forth, looking for the pesky flying thing. He grumbled and started shuffling, dragging Rhiannon, head first, along the rocky ground.

"Now, Cricket! Make him small!"

Cricket nodded. She pointed her little finger at the ogre. Her eyes gleamed and she grinned.

"BIG!" she cried, laughing.

The ogre began to shake and a thunderous growl escaped his throat. "AHHRRRGGGRAAHH!"

Then he shot into the sky.

Isabel barely had time to get her and Cricket out of the way. His big body became truly giant, swelling so that it seemed there wasn't enough room in the sky. He towered above the tallest tree, his wrinkled head reaching toward the stars. His gigantic body was now bigger than any castle tower back home.

"Cricket! I said SMALL!" Isabel scolded as she flew backwards, trying to get some perspective. The whole world had gone black and shiny. She flew higher and realized with horror that it was Kevin she was looking at. He was huge again, still curled around the ogre's monstrous, crusty toenail.

She soared into the air, up and up along the leathery hide of the giant ogre. She flew under the frayed bottom of his pants, near his scabby knees, and caught a whiff of his musky, dog smell. Then she continued, higher and higher until finally she reached his hand.

There, she saw her sister. The giant version.

Rhiannon still hung from the ogre's hand, only now she was huge. She was upside down, her body the size of an oak tree. Rhiannon's long brown hair swung below her like a hundred horse tails, and her bright green eyes glowed in the night sky like two shining stars. Angry, furious stars.

"CATELYN ALISE! SMALL!"

Her voice shook the air, pushing her sisters back as it pulsed through the sky.

Isabel flew backwards and twisted her head. "Cricket, make them small!"

Cricket hung her head and stuck her bottom lip out. She crossed her arms and glared at her sisters.

"Rhiannon!" Isabel shouted, "You hurt her feelings."

Rhiannon's huge eyes darted toward them, flashing with disbelief. "ARE YOU KIDDING?" she bellowed, blasting them backward. "She turns me into a mutant and I hurt *her* feelings?" She shook her head, sending waves through her flowing river of hair.

"Fine." She smiled through her pumpkin sized teeth. "Cricket, I'm sorry I yelled at you. Please make me small." She rolled her eyes at Isabel. "And hurry up. Before the mean ogre decides to eat me for dinner."

Cricket pointed her pudgy finger. "MALL! SS..MALL!"

Isabel dashed out of the way as the colossus combination of ogre, Rhiannon and Kevin shook. The air blurred and they shrunk to normal size, landing on the flat rock below.

Isabel dove toward them, darting into the campsite. Kevin had managed to pry his fangs loose from the ogre's toe. He was coiled in the corner, trying to stay out of the way.

Isabel landed on one of the large boulders. Cricket crawled off and waited, her finger pointed at the ogre.

"Are you okay?" Isabel shouted to Rhiannon.

Rhiannon hung limp in the confused ogre's hand. She swung herself around and glared at her sister. "Really? I'm about to be DINNER! No I'm not okay!"

"I just meant from Cricket's spell thing, that's all. Geez, Rhi!"

The ogre turned to Isabel's voice. He growled and stepped forward, bracing himself, then flung Rhiannon like a weapon, hurling her toward Isabel. She landed badly, her leg crunching against the hard rock. It lay twisted underneath her as she screamed, writhing in agony.

Isabel flew at the ogre. She kicked at his head, avenging her screaming sister. But the ogre was unfazed. He flopped a hand lazily at Isabel as she buzzed around his face. He reached up and rubbed his hairy ear, then trudged toward Rhiannon's helpless, injured body.

Rhiannon lay on the boulder, her mind clouded with pain. She could hear the ogre coming, sliding over the dusty rocks below her. Worse, she could sense how angry he was, how he was through waiting for his dinner. She knew they should run, but she doubted she could even stand. Her leg hurt more than she'd thought possible. Darkness crept in from the edges, closing on her like a blackened sky. Her screams began to fade and the pain dulled.

The last thing she saw was Cricket, sitting on top of her, growling and pointing her finger.

20

New Friends

Soft light filtered through the small tent, waking Fiona. She opened her eyes and the room began to spin. She closed them and took a deep breath. Her lungs hurt deep inside and felt heavy, like someone had dropped a sack full of grain on her chest. She got nothing but a shallow wheeze.

Ahh, yes. The debt.

Her mouth was dry and her tongue seemed huge, like a fuzzy hundred-legger had crawled in her mouth and died.

Where am I? Where's Manzy?

And then she remembered. She lay on the hard ground, her heart racing. They'd been attacked; Manzy was hurt but had gotten away, and she'd been captured by Graven.

She steadied herself, taking stock of her injuries. Waves of pain radiated from her left shoulder and into her throbbing head. Her whole body hurt, and she wondered wearily, even though she wasn't sure where she was, if going back to sleep was a better idea. She'd been dreaming, she remembered, about her mother again. The one where she was little, sitting on the floor in front of a crackling fire, while her mother brushed her hair. It had been so soothing, so real.

I have to get out of here.

She lay quietly and decided to figure it out later. She was still so tired. If she could just sleep a little longer, maybe things wouldn't be so bad when she woke up. She took a shallow breath and began to sink back into the fog, back to the place where it didn't hurt so much, back to her mother.

"Wakey, wakey," a man's voice whispered as he ducked through the tent flap.

Even half asleep she could tell he was shuffling toward her. She could hear him standing there, breathing through his mouth. She ignored him, hoping he'd go away and let her sleep. Whoever he was, he could wait. He didn't know how bad it hurt to be awake, or how bad it hurt just to breathe.

And then she felt a jarring thud through the bottom of her boot.

"Get up!" a deep voice shouted from the far end of the tent.

Before she had time to open her eyes, he kicked her again. Hard. This time in the leg, just above her knee. The motion sent waves of pain rocking through her shoulder, and she cried out in spite of herself.

"I said GET UP!" He nudged her again, this time in the ribs.

Fiona opened her eyes to a blurred vision of Wilkes. He was leaning over her, resting his hands on his knees. When he saw that she recognized him, he smiled and stood up.

Fiona blinked and as her vision cleared she saw Cal too, standing behind his partner with a stupid grin spread across his ugly, whiskered face.

"See there, Cal," Wilkes said, watching Fiona wake to her painful reality, "she just needed some encouragement."

"Yeah, yeah," Cal said, nodding his head, "that's what mum always said I needed. Ankcouragement."

Wilkes turned around. "Shut up, will ya'?"

Fiona patted the ground, her fingers searching as far as she could reach. All she needed was one block of Blast. One beautiful block of Blast and these two were history.

"What'cha' lookin' for?" Wilkes asked sweetly, catching her out of the corner of his eye. "Not that fancy bag with all the goodies, I hope." He frowned. "'Cause that's been confiscated."

Cal leaned over. "Yeah, comfisgated."

Wilkes pushed him back by the face. Then he sighed and crouched on his haunches. He smiled at Fiona.

She was wide awake now, the constant throbbing of her neck and shoulder fading as the little man closed in on her. She snapped her head to the side, sending shivers of pain through her shoulder and all along her neck.

But it was worth it, just to not look at him.

"Don't be like that," Wilkes said as she looked away. "If ya' ask me, we're meant to be friends. I mean, everywhere I turn these days, there you are! First in the King's chambers, listening to things you shouldn't hear, and then just last night, I turn around and there you are again, about to be cat food."

He grabbed Fiona by the chin, forcing her to look at him. He raised his eyebrows. "See what I mean?"

"Oh! Oh!" Cal shouted. "Don't forget Wilkes, she was with the *you know whats* when you locked them in the *you know where*." He smiled and winked.

Wilkes clenched his teeth. "Shut it, will ya'?"

He looked at Fiona and smiled. "I'm glad you made it through the night though, since we're friends." His eyes widened. "Not everyone woulda' after a fight like that." He whistled in feigned admiration. "That horse of yours didn't though," and he clucked his tongue. "Bad business, that was. Last I saw she was hobbled pretty bad and losing even more blood than you. Runnin' in circles, half crazed with the pain." His little eyes danced with delight. "Not much you can do with something in that much misery." He reached out and shoved her shoulder. "Know what I mean?"

Fiona gasped as white hot pain shot through her, threatening to knock her out. She held her breath and glared at the evil little man, refusing to cry out.

She can't be dead. He's lying. She was getting away. I saw her! She was losing a lot of blood, but it can't be true.

She pictured Manzy struggling with the cat, bleeding from the bite wounds. She could've found her way to the campsite and gotten help, she thought. Or, more likely, the dark side of her mind whispered, Wilkes is right and she wandered the mountainside, frightened and alone, until she collapsed and finally bled out.

As the reality of Manzy's death began to sink in, surrounding her like a dark fog, Fiona broke. She felt like she was suffocating, like she was drowning in desperation. She cried out, her sobs loud and wild like an injured animal.

Wilkes quickly bent down and clasped his hand over her mouth. "Keep it down," he hissed. "We wouldn't want Uncle Fancy Pants to think something's wrong, now would we?"

"Yeah, no way that horse lived," Cal said, ignoring them. "No way at all. I told Wilkes to go after her for the meat." He licked his green teeth and smiled. "But he said we had plenty of stew waiting back at camp. 'Cause just yesterday Wilkes here shot a flickerfawn! Caught her right at the edge of the Wood, too, right when she was changing. It went down real hard, thrashing and screaming, prob'ly like your horse. Wilkes says they taste better that way. Don't cha', Wilkes?"

Fiona's swollen eyes darted from Wilkes to Cal. Her breath came hard through her nose and hot tears streamed down the sides of her face. She needed a plan. She needed to focus. But all she could think about was Manzy, running through the woods, alone.

"Cal and I worked pretty hard," Wilkes said, standing up. Cal nodded enthusiastically from behind. "Late into the night. Bandaging your neck and wrapping your shoulder. Even gave you some crushed comfrey root for that cough."

"That's real bad," Cal said, shaking his head. "Mum always said a wheezing cough was real bad."

Fiona's eyes narrowed. *I'll show you what bad is, as soon as I get out of here.*

Wilkes tucked the tip of his boot under Fiona's left shoulder. "Way I see it," he said, shrugging, "you owe us. Ferront might've shot that cat, but we're who doctored you. Plus," and he leered down at her with a greasy smile, "now we're friends."

He stood for a second, his eyes locked on hers as he let the truth of her situation sink in. "And now," he said smiling, "I hear you've been up to no good. Kidnapping? My my," he said, clucking his tongue, "that does sound serious."

"Yeah, Wilkes," Cal said, "kidnapping *is* serious. No one's safe, if ya' think about it. Kinda scary, really."

"So now that you're good and rested," Wilkes said, "as your friend, I'm asking you nicely. GET. UP." And with each word he shoved on her very broken shoulder with his boot.

Fiona screamed, her body betraying her to the pain. Her eyes clenched as she caught her breath. Cold sweat dripped from her forehead and when she opened her eyes again, they began to water.

"I'm sorry," Wilkes said, shaking his head as he hitched up his pants, "my foot slipped." He laughed and headed toward the tent flap. When Wilkes reached the door he looked at Fiona, lying helpless and crying softly on the floor.

"Oh," he said, smiling. "I almost forgot. News came round camp this mornin' about that fairy friend of yours. Thought I'd pass it along. Least I could do, ya' know, since we're friends."

Fiona's eyes flickered, desperate for word of Jaydin. Her chest heaved and she caught her breath.

It'll kill him when I tell him about Manzy.

Wilkes shrugged his shoulders. "I'm afraid while you was runnin' from us, justice was served." He ran his finger across his throat and smiled. "The fairy's dead."

He ducked through the tent flap and walked away, his laughter ringing in Fiona's ears.

21

Foo

"There's a small stream ahead," Kevin said as he slid in front of Manzy, "in close proximity to the trail. Though it will be hard," he said, rolling his eyes, "to smell over the stench of that *thing*. We can refresh there."

"Sounds good," Manzy said, pawing the ground. She looked across the trail to where the girls stood, huddled around Cricket, and sighed. It had been hard to convince them to go home, to abandon the quest for Annis, but she and Kevin had managed it. With Fiona undoubtedly headed for the Tower, it seemed the right move. Besides, Kevin had explained, if Graven and his henchmen got in their way, Cricket could unleash her frighteningly powerful finger and shrink them, just like she'd done with her new pet.

Cricket twirled in the tall weeds beside the trail, making the ogre fly like a tiny glider. Well, a tiny angry glider.

Last night, as the ogre had been about to pounce, Cricket had shrunk him to the size of a chipmunk. Isabel had wanted to fling him across the mountain like a piece of trash, but Cricket had reached out, bouncing and smiling.

"Foo! Foo!" she'd cried.

Isabel had squinted in disgust, holding him by the back of his neck like one of Cricket's old diapers. He'd kicked and growled, but in the end seemed pretty harmless. So she'd handed him to Cricket, watching to see if the little girl was going to squish him, or maybe even eat him.

Cricket had held the ogre before her chubby face and laughed. "FOO!" she'd yelled, blowing back his tiny tufts of ear hair.

"Fine, Cricket," Isabel had said, shaking her head, "but keep that thing away from me. And if I were you, I wouldn't let Rhi even see him."

The ogre had done nothing but whine and growl for food ever since. "FOO!" he'd demanded at all hours, rubbing his round little belly. "FOO!"

And though Cricket had found him a few grasshoppers and some berries, he'd only spit them back in her face and howled like an angry little puppy.

Last night Manzy had seen Cricket nuzzle him to her chest, holding him face down with her arm, trying to make him fall asleep. And even after he bit her, Cricket had laughed and moved him to the ground, where he finally fell asleep, curled up with her pudgy little hand as a blanket.

I doubt her lady mother would approve of this, Manzy thought as she stood with Kevin. She watched as Foo crouched on Cricket's hand, growling at Rhiannon.

Manzy blew through her nostrils and shook the road dust from her hide. In truth, they were beyond worrying over the Queen's favor. They'd all be lucky just to make it home. And now they were splitting up. It was a bad idea.

She stretched, careful not to pull on her wounds. Her flank still ached, but it was improving. Isabel had done a good job cleaning her up the night before. The girl had a real knack with that sort of thing; she was an instinctual nurturer. She'd rinsed the bite marks with water from the canteens and then sealed them with melted wax. It wasn't perfect, but it was all they'd had. And it was working. The bleeding had all but stopped. Which was good. They had a long walk ahead of them before they got to the castle. Before she got to Fiona.

She still had no idea what she'd find when she got there.

The best she could hope was that Fiona was being held in the Tower for kidnapping. At least then she'd be alive.

Losing her to the King's men was still better than losing her to that Spotted Cat.

She'd been telling herself that for hours. It seemed to play in her head like a minstrel's tune, over and over. It'd been there as she'd hobbled back to camp last night, wounded and alone. Then again as she passed the sleepless night, worrying for Fiona.

The girls headed toward her and Kevin. Time to go.

Rhiannon seemed improved this morning. She was still limping, but her color looked better. Last night Manzy had found her pale and chilled, resting in the corner of the rocks. In the end, she'd suffered a badly bruised leg and had the wind knocked out of her, but she'd been fine.

Losing Fiona to the King's men was better than losing her to that Spotted Cat, her mind repeated.

Or was it?

Graven's banner had been flying alongside Ferront's. The wind whipped fabric of his sigil had snapped in the moonlight as they'd taken Fiona and rode off, those ugly birds circling overhead as if they were alive, biding their time until the girl took her last breath.

If by some miracle Fiona was still alive, Manzy thought, for how long? How long until Graven put a quick end to her for what she knew? It wouldn't be hard to make it look like she'd died of her injuries.

Maybe she already has.

And, of course, there was still the debt. Every second that ticked by without payment was killing her.

No matter which way you twisted it, Manzy thought, this time Fiona was in way over her head. And *she* was stuck out here, in the middle of the mountains, with the princesses and a reeking miniature mountain ogre, limping her way to the castle.

"All set?" Kevin asked, smiling up at Manzy.

"Are you sure you don't want to ride?" Manzy asked, looking at Rhiannon.

The princess shook her head. "I'm sure. Take Cricket and go. Isabel and I want to have a look around and meet you later. It won't take long."

"Yeah," Isabel said cheerfully, "we're just going to reco, reco..,"

"Reconnoiter," Kevin interjected.

"Maybe there's something we can see from the sky that'll help find Annis," Isabel said.

"Even after we explain to Father that Jaydin and Fiona are innocent," Rhiannon said, "there's still Brent to worry about. If Caelia's right, finding Annis is the only way to release him from the Carapacem Spell. Besides," she said, tossing her head toward Kevin, "we've got him."

"A real spy," Isabel said.

"Anyway," Rhiannon laughed, "I want to see Fiona's face when she hears we went after Annis."

"In truth," Kevin began, "there are no assault plans. Just reconnaissance."

"I know, I know."

"Well then," Manzy said, as Rhiannon settled Cricket on her back, "we should go. We'll meet at the stream in a few hours. But by the Angels, be careful!"

"FOO!" the ogre barked, standing on Cricket's lap. Cricket pulled a muddy worm from under the sleeve of her dress.

"FOO! FOO!" he bellowed at the sight of it. He ran forward and kicked her hand, fighting for the worm. Cricket laughed and picked him up. He shook his head and sat down on her palm, growling.

"FOO! FOO!"

"Perhaps you could silence that acquaintance of yours," Kevin shouted to her, scrunching his face in irritation. "His overwhelming odor is lamentable enough. I'm certain Manzanita will not want him assaulting her ears as well."

Cricket nodded and cupped her hand over Foo's head, and accidentally pushed him to his knees. He growled and bit her.

"Ow!" she cried.

When she opened her hand, the little ogre was dangling from her finger, hanging by his two tiny tusks. Cricket winced and flicked him across his legs, but he refused to let go. She glared at him. With her free hand she pinched him on either side of his head. When that didn't work she squeezed his whole body until he could barely breathe, until his leathery hide turned a hazy shade of blue.

Then he let go.

The girls laughed and Kevin nodded in approval. "Quite so, lass!"

Cricket held Foo by the head and examined her bitten hand. Two little wounds, no bigger than matching beestings, dotted her finger. They'd barely even broken the skin. But they hurt.

She held Foo in front of her face and growled, low and menacing. She glared at him and rumbled deep in her throat. They stared at each other, facing off; the fierce little princess versus the vicious pet ogre.

He kicked and threw punches with his muscled little arms, scowling up at her. She held him on either side of his head and kept growling, right in his face, until finally, he looked away and went limp.

"Foo?" he asked, almost nicely, as Manzanita started down the trail.

"Foo," Cricket answered with a smile, and plopped the worm in front of him.

22

Awakenings

Fiona lay in the tent, her knees pulled to her chest, and sobbed. Manzy and Jaydin were gone. She sniffed, her labored breath ragged, and for the first time thanked the Angels for the debt. Before long she would be gone too.

Manzy was the only family she'd ever known, aside from Dee and Mickey. But Manzy had come first. After Fiona had been found, abandoned on the banks of the Winding River as an infant, the Bright Eyes had adopted her as one of their own.

She could remember sleeping in Boswell's nest as a small child, how the sticks had prickled her soft, naked skin until the old eagle had shown pity and feathered the inside for her, how the inky blackness of the sky had enveloped her each night, how she'd fallen asleep to the baying of the wolves and the coyotes, and the haunting, mournful sound of the tawny owl. How she'd felt wild and safe, all at the same time.

She'd grown under the protection of the Bright Eyes, playing with hordes of nattering squirrels and rabbits, learning to walk by gripping the fluffy white tail of a flickerfawn. And on her first nameday they'd held a beautiful ceremony pairing her with a young foal named Manzanita Rose. She'd met

Jaydin on that day. The three had been inseparable ever since.

But despite her friendships and the welcome the Bright Eyes had given her, she'd never been able to shake the feeling that something was missing, that she didn't really fit. She felt it when Caelia embraced Jaydin, or when Boswell's eyes gleamed with pride as his fledgling eagles soared for the first time. She'd always thought it was the worst.

Now she knew better.

Something inside her had broken when Wilkes told her that Manzy was dead. That Jaydin was dead, too. All the color had drained from the world. She was worthless without them.

She closed her eyes and wished *she* would just be dead, wished that the debt would come due and this insufferable sorrow would end.

Wilkes had told her, her mind whispered.

Fiona's eyes snapped open. Wilkes was a horrible little man, she thought, nothing but swamp trash. He was also a liar.

She lay quiet, her mind buzzing. If Manzy were really dead, she thought, surely she would've felt *something*. She didn't know what, exactly, but the more she considered it, the more she knew it was true. Why hadn't she thought of this before? Your life's match didn't just die without you knowing. She smiled. Manzy was still alive. She had to be. She felt it in her bones.

And if Wilkes would lie about Manzy, what's to say he hadn't lied about Jaydin? Hadn't Isabel said the King's brother, Ferront, was convinced of Jaydin's innocence, that he'd been trying to persuade the King to release the fairy?

Fiona's smile deepened and she nodded to herself. *That's exactly what she'd said.* The sharp pain in her neck reminded her that despite this new turn of events, she was still quite injured.

She laughed. Her neck hurt, her shoulder was undoubtedly broken, and she could barely breathe. Heaven's Gate, her whole body was beaten and dying, but it was nothing compared to the pain of losing Manzy and Jaydin. Now that there was a chance they were still alive, she felt like she could do anything.

I have to get out of here.

If Manzy is alive, she thought, she's still hurt. She'd seen that for herself.

She'll be moving slowly, if at all. And she needs me. I've got thistleberry salve in my pack, if Wilkes and Cal hadn't completely thrashed it, and there was a good chance Dee had sent some catgut and bone needles for stitching.

Fiona rolled herself over, ignoring the throbbing aches coming from all directions, and reached for the bottom of the tent flap. She lifted it slightly and peeked under.

Outside her tent a few horses were tied to the surrounding trees. They stood patiently, enjoying a bit of rest before the long day ahead. Men she didn't recognize were walking about, packing up and readying themselves for the day's ride. One man was squatting near the small campfire. She watched as he poured a bucket of water on it, its dying embers hissing and sending tendrils of steam and smoke into the morning air.

In the distance she saw a handsome man in leather riding boots and breeches talking to someone in a hooded black cloak. She didn't know either of them, but she was pretty sure they were having an argument. The one in breeches shook his head and pointed a finger at the other, demanding something. The other shoved something at him, a bundle of sorts.

MY PACK!

Even from this far away Fiona recognized McClane's handiwork. The green canvas bag was covered on one side with burned dots; scorch marks from Demon's Tongue. The old man had probably stored the canvas too close to his detonation zone again.

Get my pack. Then find Manzy.

The man in breeches turned and walked swiftly toward her tent. The other followed, and as he raised his head from under the black hood she realized it was Graven.

"Perhaps the contents would be useful, your Grace," she heard Graven say, trailing behind the other.

"The contents of the girl's pack are evidence," the man said, "and are not to be toyed with. I will not have my nieces' safety jeopardized by your curiosity. Enough, Graven. Take it up with my brother when we reach the castle."

"Indeed, your Grace."

Fiona watched as Graven slipped into a neighboring tent. The man in breeches, who could only be Ferront, Fiona thought, continued past her tent until he was out of view. For a minute she could hear him, his black leather boots cracking over the twigs and underbrush of the forest as he walked. And then he was gone, her pack along with him.

She let the bottom edge of the tent fabric fall from her hand and rolled onto her back. This would not be easy. She sighed, and began to form a plan. She inhaled slowly, testing the limits of her sickened, failing lungs. Her throat tightened unexpectedly, and she coughed. She rolled onto her stomach to stifle the noise, not wanting anyone to know she was awake, and bumped her broken shoulder. She was instantly overcome by a wave of nausea.

She lay still until it passed then slowly raised her head. The blanket under her was stained dark with blood. From her injuries or her cough, she couldn't tell. She wiped her mouth with the back of her hand and found fresh blood. Her hands, she realized as she wiped the bright red blood on her vest, had turned an ugly, ashy shade of grey.

Not good.

Get out first, she thought. Get your pack. Find Manzy. All that without being able to breathe. For that matter, she realized, she may not even be able to stand. She crawled to her knees, painfully, and was about to attempt it, when her eyes lit with a thought. She had no need to stand. She rolled onto her back, silently thanked the Angels for Caelia, and whispered *Assurgam*.

23

Loose Ends

Graven liked his chambers dark, preferring the dim glow of a few candles to any natural light. The heavy, velvet curtains that lined the tall windows were rarely opened. But tonight was an exception.

The Blood Moon had risen, a deep scarlet orb in the night sky, and Graven took it as a good omen. Not only had the Thorn girl died of her injuries, but Wilkes and Cal had seen to the body, burying her somewhere in the woods. The royal search party had come back to the castle empty handed, and so much the better.

Graven stood by the windows, his back to the room, smiling as he gazed at the moon's ominous beauty. And if the dangers of the wilderness could kill the older girl, he thought, it would certainly work its deadly charms on the younger, more fragile princesses. He sighed, contented that these annoying loose ends had resolved themselves so cleanly, leaving little to worry over. Only the fairy and the King.

Cal watched his boss turn from the windows and walk closer, the flames from the scattered candelabras wavering in Graven's wake. He was smiling, Cal noticed, which was good. It could be a trap, though. Either way, lying to the old man had been a bad idea, like playing chicken with a Thicket Viper. But Wilkes had said it was for the best. When they'd found the Thorn girl's tent empty that morning, he'd promised she wouldn't get far, promised she'd just die anyway, sick as she was, and that the old man would never have to know she'd escaped. Wilkes said Graven would even thank them for taking care of it, that they'd be doin' him a favor.

As Graven sat down behind his writing table, Cal shivered and hoped his partner had been right. Two fat candles on the desk lit up the old man's face from underneath, making him even more gaunt and eerie than usual.

Every time Cal had been here it'd been like this, dark and full of shadows. The kind of dark that seemed like it could swallow you up. As he sat across from his boss, even with Wilkes right beside him, it was the same as usual. Creepy. His eyes followed the flickering candlelight as it cast shadows about the room. It danced across the curtains, making him think of giant ghosts floating toward him. It flickered on the walls and high on the ceiling in scary, moving shapes, just like the phantoms that sometimes haunted his dreams.

But most of all, it lit up the caged vulture beside Graven. The bird was enormous, almost as big as a child, only more menacing. It rested inside the large metal cage, its sharp talons wrapped around a twisted branch. The dim shadows wavered around the bird, and whenever its black eyes glinted in the eerie light, Cal thought it was staring at him, whispering the truth about the Thorn girl to its master.

The whole thing was distracting for him, and dangerous too. He knew he should be listening. The old man was right there behind the table, twisting his big ring back and forth and talking about something. The plan probably. But Cal couldn't focus. It was too dark, with too many shadows for things to hide in. And anyway, he didn't like being this close to the old man. He slouched and fidgeted, wishing the chair had arms. Wishing they could get out of here.

"Hey Cal," Wilkes said, jabbing him in the arm, "want a muffin?"

"Huh?" he asked, looking over at his partner. Wilkes was holding a small woven basket out to him. It was draped with a red and white checked cloth and inside were two big muffins. "Yeah, thanks," he said, smiling as he reached toward the basket.

"Don't be stupid, will ya?" Wilkes said, yanking the basket out of his reach. "You got a deathwish or somethin'?" He covered the muffins with the checked cloth and put the basket on the floor. "These are the ones boss was talkin' about. The special *homemade* ones."

"Oh," Cal said, nodding, though he had no idea what Wilkes was talking about.

"I don't care how you do it," Graven said, his silky voice sliding through the room, "just finish it. Tonight." The candlelight glinted in his dark eyes, making Cal think he looked just like his ugly bird. "As for the other," Graven said, holding his left hand out in front of him as he admired his sigil ring, "I'll take care of that."

"But boss?" Wilkes asked, "what about the princesses?"

"Everyone believes the Thorn girl left them to die in the tunnels," Graven answered, smiling at the men, "thanks to the *confession* she gave you before she died so tragically of her injuries."

"But Wilkes, where'd they really go?" Cal asked. "Those kids saw us, they saw our faces."

"It doesn't matter," Graven said. "Three little girls, out there," and he gestured to the windows, "on their own? They've either run as far north as the Ringing Trees, or, if we're lucky, they're dead." His mouth twitched in a small smile. "And if they do come crawling back, no one will believe a word they say."

"Not even the King, boss? I think he would believe his own kids."

"Not unless he can do it from the grave. And Wilkes?"

"Yeah, boss?"

"Leave the thinking to me."

Graven reached for a rolled scroll on the table, and with a flick of his wrist dismissed the men. He unrolled the parchment and began reading, but as Wilkes and Cal were just through the door he said, "Leave one."

Cal hesitated, frightened. Was this the trap? Had the old man known they'd been lying about the girl the whole time and now one of them had to stay for punishment? It would be him, too. He just knew it. The old man would probably decide to keep him in a cage, like his creepy bird, or maybe he'd even feed him to the stupid bird. This was bad. Real bad, he thought, slithering behind Wilkes. If only he knew what the old man was talking about.

But Wilkes knew what Graven wanted. He tipped his head in apology and handed the basket back to the old man. "Sorry, sir."

Graven's mouth twisted in irritation. He removed one of the poisoned muffins from the basket and wrapped it in a separate cloth. When he handed the basket back to Wilkes, he was smiling. The young man relaxed as he headed outside with Cal. He assumed the smile was for him.

It wasn't. Graven sat behind the large table for sometime after the two imbeciles had gone, smiling into the darkness. His eyes gleamed with hope for the future. A future where he was King, crowned in the aftermath of the tragic death of their current sovereign. When the people of Amryn saw what he had done for them, it would happen. No one, not even Ferront, would have a claim as strong as his own. When they realized he had avenged the Neulock boy by putting the villainous fairy to death, that he was the one who had finally put an end to their suffering by punishing the guilty, they would thank him.

And when he brought the royal seamstress, Delia, before them, shackled and shamed, they would thank him too. How exquisitely convenient he had recognized her that morning on the coast. He would explain, with a practiced tear and a sad shake of his head, how her heart had been so filled with hatred after the Thorn girl's capture, how she'd become deranged with the thought that the girl had died at the hands of the crown, that she'd poisoned their great King with nothing less than Shadowbells, secreting them into the castle, deep within her sewing basket. How she had ever managed to get them into the innocent looking muffins, he would say with a sigh, we may never know. But the sewing basket, he will tell them, full of the deadly flowers, speaks for itself. They will thank him for securing their safety and punishing the evil murderer.

And then they will crown him.

Perhaps then, he thought as his bony fingers caressed the carved surface of his ring, when he is King, he could be rid of the rest of the fairies and the filthy Bright Eyes in the castle as well. The future was bright and filled with hope. And luckily, he thought with a wicked smile, just around the corner.

****

Roland was new at his job, and while he liked his uncle Bo very much, his dreams did not include working as a Tower guard. What he wanted, more than anything, was to apprentice in the kitchens with Mistress Brandywine.

All of his brothers and most of his friends teased him about it. They laughed and said he was foolish, that if he got his way he would never see any more of the kingdom than the inside of a steaming kitchen. But none of them had been anywhere outside of Amryn either, and so he ignored them. They called him Sir Spatula and the Noodle Knight. But he didn't care.

To spend his days before the great flaming hearths, baking breads and sweet pastries, or turning a pile of flour and eggs into the most tender pasta the King had ever tasted? That was his path. To be able to cook for the King, he thought, as he leaned against the outside of the Tower under the glow of the Blood Moon, that would be something.

At almost fourteen, he was a real oddity, nothing like the other boys his age. He was very happy to leave the horses and swords to others. And that made his mother worry. So much, in fact, that while she wanted him to be happy, she also thought he could use a man's guidance. Someone to toughen him up and help fill the space left by his dead father. And so, instead of apprenticing with Mistress Brandywine, like he wanted, he was here, working for his uncle Bo.

Roland's eyes lit up and he looked around. It was dark, and though the moon was full, it was still hard to see. But darkness had no effect on his sense of smell. He sniffed a few times, then inhaled deeply, searching for the source of the sugary scent wafting under his nose. He wasn't sure where it was coming from, but somewhere was the delicious smell of freshly baked muffins.

And then he saw them coming. The man carrying the basket was short and stocky, like his big brother Chet. He was smiling as he approached, but in a way that put Roland in mind of the foxes that hid behind his mother's barn sometimes, trying to get at the hens. As they got closer, Roland realized that the man walked like Chet too, chest first, with his big arms at his sides.

The other one was much taller and it took a minute for Roland to absorb his appearance. It was, after all, the first time he'd ever seen a fairy. He knew most folks didn't care for them, his brothers certainly didn't, but he thought the skinny creature was fantastic. A bit uglier than he would've expected, it was true. And if he was honest, the greenish look to its teeth was kind of disturbing. Other than that, he guessed it seemed alright. It had the same clothes as any man, except its pants were rolled up to the knee, and it had pointed shoes. They were very bright and matched the shade of pink splotches in its small wings perfectly. At least from what he could see. It was hard to get a good look at them, it being so dark and all.

"What can I do for you?" Roland asked nervously as they approached. Not only was it the first time he'd encountered a fairy, it was also the first time anyone had bothered to notice him at all while he was on duty.

"We've brought sweets," the one like Chet said, casting a forlorn glance up at the Tower, "for my friend's doomed relation." He held the basket up for inspection.

"I see that!" Roland said. He smiled approvingly at the handsome red and white checked cloth. Not everyone would've taken such care. "I could smell those muffins halfway across the road! You must've put a lot of love in those."

"Yes," the short one said with a sad smile, "they're very special."

Roland reached toward the basket like he was about to touch a priceless piece of art. "May I?"

"Not a good idea," the fairy said in a high pitched, squeaky voice, shaking his ugly head.

The short one looked up at his friend and patted him on the arm. Roland thought it was a bit harder than necessary, but then, he knew how rough friends and brothers could be.

"Go ahead," the short one said, "I bet you have to be sure there isn't anything dangerous in there!" He laughed, a deep throaty chuckle.

"True enough," Roland answered, flipping open the checked cloth. He leaned forward, and sticking his face close to the basket, he inhaled. "Mmmm," he said as he stood back up. "They smell wonderful." He gently covered the muffins, tucking the cloth inside as if it were covering a sleeping baby. "There are more rules than you could imagine in a place like this. And unfortunately," he said, shrugging his shoulders, "one of them is visitors are allowed on Sundays only."

The fairy began to sob. Softly at first, then louder, until he was wailing so hard it was beginning to attract attention from a group of villagers passing by.

"It's just that," the one like Chet began in a low whisper, "his brother is up there, and we don't know when, well, if, he'll ever get out. And, besides," he finished with a quick wink, "the muffins won't keep 'til Sunday."

The fairy leaned over and loudly blew his nose behind his friend's back. The stocky man grimaced and punched the fairy in the side. Hard, too.

But Roland understood. His brothers loved to rub all kinds of boogies and disgusting stuff on him when he wasn't looking. He felt like punching them a lot.

"I'll tell you what I can do," he said, happy to be able to oblige these folks and keep to the letter of the law as well. "I'll deliver the basket for you."

"Thank you," the short one said, bowing slightly. "You'd be doing us such a service."

"Good!" Roland said, and clapped his hands together, pleased with how the whole thing was turning out.

The short one smiled as he handed over the basket of muffins, and Roland thought of the fox again. He watched them walk across the dirt road until they melted back into the darkness. Roland shrugged his shoulders, dismissing any small sense of anxiety the man's twisted smile had caused. After all, how bad could someone who delivered fresh, homemade muffins really be?

24

The Bitter Mountains

Fiona leaned over and grabbed another handful of snow. Her bare fingers burned with the cold, but she had to get rid of the sour taste in her mouth. She nibbled on the icy ball until she could no longer taste her own vomit.

She stood crunching the last of the ice and smirked. Anyone tracking her would have plenty to follow; lots of icy piles of puke. She imagined the look on Rhiannon's face and laughed out loud, her voice muffled by the falling snow. The girl wasn't so bad, she supposed, in small doses.

She sighed. Perhaps chewing on the comfrey root had been a bad idea.

She'd found the woody stalk that morning, lying on a pile of bloody bandages as she'd slipped outside her tent. She'd grabbed it and counted herself lucky, knowing it would aid her failing lungs. And it had. It had also made her throw up every quarter hour. She knew comfrey root was supposed to be crushed and dissolved in a draught, but that took time and patience. She'd had neither.

After she'd quietly reclaimed her pack from where it'd been tied to one of the horses, she'd zipped over the foothills, searching for Manzy. She'd looked everywhere, scanning the forest for tracks or a blood trail; anything at all. But there'd been nothing. She'd even returned to the girls' campsite, hoping to find someone, but it'd been empty. She'd stood in the middle of the camp, confused by the rubble, and disappointed, weighing her options.

She could go back to the castle and beg for Jaydin's release, for help finding Manzy. Manzy was well respected, known by many Bright Eye members on the King's Council. There was a chance they would help. But she wasn't just a trouble maker in the King's eyes any more. She was a criminal, a kidnapper. Not to mention Graven would be lurking at every turn. Without the princesses to back her up, going anywhere near the castle was suicide.

She could wander the foothills, looking for Manzy. She could spend days searching, trying in some blind, hopeful way to help. But it would be the last thing she did, for when the small bit of comfrey root ran out she knew her time would be measured in hours and minutes, not days. There are worse ways to end a life, she'd thought, standing in the destroyed campsite, caressing the key around her neck.

And yet, there was Annis.

She'd cursed the boy. She'd set the whole thing in motion, Fiona felt sure of it. The Moonshadow had shown her the old clawed fairy as the way to save Jaydin. She'd likely pay for that information with her life. It'd be a shame not to use it.

The best way to end a life, she'd thought as she whispered *assurgam* and headed for the Bitter Mountains, is with the truth. She meant to find it.

By midday she'd left the foothills behind. The mountain air had become cold, the trees less varied. She'd rested near the first peak, snuggling inside her cloak against the chill. Even though she'd been nauseous she'd made herself nibble on a dried out piece of gingercake she'd found in the side of her pack. Caelia hadn't mentioned how much levitating wore you out, and she'd needed the energy. She'd been weary, tired to her very bones, but moved on, hoping she'd get a little benefit from the sweet bread before it inevitably came back up.

By early evening she'd made the second peak, high enough to find the snow. The first flakes were fat and soft, landing on her cheeks like a feather's kiss. Now her cheeks burned with the cold, when she could feel them at all. The higher she'd gotten, the harder the cursed snow fell. And the wind had picked up, too, blowing the storm nearly sideways in places. The trees had quickly become lumpy, snow covered pillars, the rocky outcroppings nothing but shadowy mounds of white.

She'd been forced to spend the last hour walking as well, her power of levitation gone after the food ran out. It was grueling, exhausting work, even on a good day. Her pack felt heavier than she'd remembered, her shoulder screaming with every step as she'd forged a painful, slow path through the knee high snow. She'd made some ground, she thought, but it was hard to be sure. For all she knew she might be walking in circles; the snow covered her tracks as soon as she'd even made them.

She stood now, her hands on her knees, shivering, trying to recover. The coughing had come back with a vengeance. This time, she realized with fear, there were small dark clots in the snow, along with the bright red sprays of blood.

That's new.

She wretched, fear twisting in her belly, and wiped her face. Puking every quarter hour had been better than this. She laughed, a sad, empty sound, and allowed herself another minute of rest. She stared blankly into the night. Nothing but snow and the ugly, rasping sound of her wheezing. Her throat had begun to close as well, there was no use denying it. There'd been a few times when she'd felt as if her breath was coming from too far away, through nothing larger than a hollow reed.

This had been folly, she thought. She should've stayed in the foothills and looked for Manzy. But here, she had no idea where she was, or worse, where she was going. Her food was gone and she had nothing more than a thin wool cloak to warm her. And with the last of the comfrey root gone, the nausea was over, but her breath would continue to worsen. This time for good. If only she knew where she was going.

Three times as high and onward go.

Foster's words spun in her head. She'd been repeating them all day, hoping their meaning would unravel. Three times as high as what?

She looked at the sky, marveling at how the falling snow nearly blocked the Blood Moon. She took heart; a Blood Moon was rare and lucky.

~ 162 ~

She wrapped her cloak tighter, trying to hold some warmth in, and winced. The comfrey root had done nothing for her broken shoulder or the wound in her neck. The truth was, she was more than exhausted. She was dying. Nothing could save her now, short of finding a way to pay the debt. Still, it wasn't too late for Manzy and Jaydin, or the Neulock boy.

If she could just find Annis. But even if she did, she thought as she sunk to the cold ground, leaning against the closest boulder, she had no idea what to do. She was in no shape to fight anyone, let alone a bitter fairy with an enchanted flute. The whole thing was beginning to seem impossible. In truth, it had all been a bit impossible from the start. She looked into the darkness, mesmerized by the curtain of snow fall, and thought how good it would feel to finally lay down, to just stop.

She closed her eyes and pictured her and her mother inside a cottage, cozy and warm before a fire, the smell of baking bread in the air. It was snowing, a heavy, late winter storm, and her father, always a little like McClane in these fantasies, bursts through the door, his cheeks rosy with the cold, a bundle of wood in his strong arms.

"How are my girls," he asks, stacking the wood by the fire. Her mother takes his wet cloak, hangs it on the handsome iron hook by the door that he and Fiona had made as a present for her last Savior's Day, and hands him a steaming mug of spiced mead. She settles herself by the fire and sips from her own drink, her eyes smiling at Fiona over the mug.

"You're home now," her mother says, "get yourself good and warm."

Fiona opened her eyes, her frigid hands wrapped around an imaginary mug of cider.

She knew nothing of them, really. All of her imaginary scenarios were just that—imaginary. She didn't know how they'd looked or sounded, how they'd laughed or what foods they'd longed for. She didn't even know how or why they'd died. Worse, she didn't know if they'd even loved her. The only thing she knew for certain was that they'd left her, alone on the banks of the Winding River, that they'd given her away. She had nothing from her parents but the key, found with her that day by the Bright Eyes.

It won't be so bad, she thought. She felt through her tunic for the familiar metal, as much a part of her as her own skin. At least then I'll get some answers.

Fight Fiona! Don't give up on me!

Manzy's words echoed in her mind. She pictured her, circling her and the Spotted Cat yesterday, striking out with her front feet, fighting, never giving up. Her life's match was still out there. And she needed her. Jaydin needed her. She shook her head, as if she could fling the traitorous thoughts of surrender into the wind, and reminded herself what had to be done.

She crawled to her feet and decided she must've reached the third and last peak of the mountain by now. But the snow was falling so thick and heavy you couldn't tell one direction from another. It was dizzying, blinding.

Through wretched cold and blinding snow.

She leaned against the closest outcropping to get out of the wind and squinted, trying to discern the best path.

Movement, up ahead.

Her heart began to race. Had Graven been tracking her after all? Or was it Ferront and the King's men?

But that was madness. No one came up here. It was probably just a Cottonjack, hoping for something green to eat. But Cottonjacks can't live at this altitude, she thought, and there's been nothing green around for hours. She pressed herself against the cold stone and tried to be still, to be ready for whatever was out there.

Had Annis sensed her coming? Was the old fairy hunting *her*? Fiona hadn't considered that. She waited, her heart pounding, desperate to glean a clue from the darkness.

But there was nothing. After what seemed like forever her heart slowed. She trudged forward again, her feet crunching through the icy top crust, convinced the darkness and the falling snow had been playing tricks with her eyes.

Had she not almost stepped in the hole, she would've missed him.

"Look at you!" she said, leaning over to investigate. Trapped in a deep tube of snow was a spider the size of a small pup. By the look of things, it'd fallen off the ridge above and landed backwards; its hairy legs pressed against its body so tightly it couldn't move.

And from the bright red color of its eyes it was undoubtedly a Snow Spider. His big, frightened eyes glowed in the night. She'd never seen one in real life before. From all the wild tales she'd heard, she'd expected them to be bigger. She shrugged her shoulders and moved on, content to leave the spider as it was. Snow Spiders were vicious, no matter their size, fiercely territorial and regarded as one of the most dangerous creatures in the kingdom. She had enough to worry over without adding a venomous bite to the list.

She'd not gotten ten paces before turning around. She couldn't just leave him there to starve. Yes, she reminded herself as she headed back, this was a bad idea. She smiled. She could almost hear the disapproving tone in Manzy's voice telling her the same.

The spider was exactly as she'd left him, still trapped backwards in the hole. In the bottom of her pack, under a few blocks of Blast, she found what she needed. She grabbed the slender stick of Angel's Breath by the fuse and eased it out of her pack.

"Easy does it," she whispered, carefully using the blunt end of the explosive to widen the hole. Had they not been surrounded by snow she'd never have attempted such a thing. Angel's Breath had a way of getting away from you, even with a long fuse.

The spider watched as she dug through the snow, his red eyes following her every move. When his legs were finally freed, he stretched them, testing each one in turn.

Fiona crouched by the hole, fascinated by the hairy little thing, waiting for him to move on. He was kind of cute, in a poisonous, creepy sort of way. But as the spider began to crawl out, she stood and backed away, remembering his reputation.

Without warning she lost her breath.

It was sudden and unexpected, like she'd been kicked in the chest or had the wind knocked out of her. One minute she could breathe, the next she could not.

She fell to her knees, struggling, punching the snow as she fought for any sip of air. She fell to her side, her mouth gaping open like a fish out of water, and wondered if this was how it would end. How she would end. She remembered nearly drowning the day before yesterday, how her chest had burned, how she'd been desperate to reach the surface and devour the crisp air. Somehow, this was worse. She was surrounded by air and still couldn't breathe.

Collapsed in the snow, oblivious to the wet and the cold and the spider that was slowly crawling toward her hand, she wanted nothing more than to breathe, to fill her empty lungs with fresh, cold air. She'd seen lungs before, had hunted with McClane enough times to recognize one organ from another. She imagined hers now as leaden lumps of grey in her chest, pinning her to the ground, dragging her to her death.

And then, it was over. As suddenly as it had gone, her breath returned. She gasped loudly, filling her lungs with delicious air, more grateful than she'd ever been in all her fourteen years. She lay slumped in the snow, breathing, promising herself that if there was a way out of this mess, she'd find it. Somehow she would find Annis, she would pay the debt, and she would make sure she never had to go through that again.

She sat up, slowly feeling more her old self, and noticed the baby spider. He was beside her, exploring the forgotten stick of Angel's Breath with his two front legs.

"That's not a toy," she mumbled, crawling to her feet. She swished at him, hoping to send him on his way. He jumped back and hissed.

"Don't be like that," she said. She leaned forward, carefully reaching for the explosive, and crossed her fingers that he would be frightened off by her size. She could almost hear McClane, scolding her for fooling around with Angel's Breath. She needed to secure that stick.

But the spider wouldn't budge. She huffed, took off her pack, reached in and tore a small hunk of Glow from a larger wad. She kneaded it back and forth until it began to give off a bright yellow light.

Glow never hurt anybody, she thought, and threw it at the spider. It hit him on the thickest part of his abdomen, sliding him sideways. He shook his head, grabbed the stick of Angel's Breath he'd claimed, and took off across the top of the snow, his pudgy little body glowing bright yellow in the darkness.

"Hey!" Fiona called, "I need that!" She chased after him, her pack forgotten in the snow, and tried to follow the fading yellow light. "I know, Mick," she mumbled as she ran, "I know. But I wasn't exactly fooling around."

25

Web of Lies

The cave was dark and it took Fiona a second to adjust her eyes. She'd followed the spider, hoping to find her stick of Angel's Breath, and found the old fairy instead. Annis sat on the other side of the room in a chair made of ice, holding the Sarastro in her lap.

"Fiona," she said, her smile cracking the frozen crust around her mouth. Ice chips tinkled on the frozen floor below. "I've been waiting for you."

A black cauldron churned along the left wall, warmed by flames underneath. An eerie white light came from inside. It glinted on the wet surfaces of the cave and lit the room in a ghostly glow.

Fiona stood near the entrance to the cave, wheezing, her hands on her knees, trying to figure out what to do. Five minutes ago she'd been outside, playing around with a Snow Spider, and now she was here, in front of the old fairy.

This is bad, Fiona thought, looking around. The whole place was crawling with spiders. Snow Spiders. Webs twisted across the low ceiling and hung from every inch of ice, the gossamer threads bouncing along the walls as the spiders crept from one shadowy corner to the other, their red eyes dancing in the darkness.

Fiona reached for her pack, knowing she'd feel better with some Blast in her hands, and tried to think of a plan.

My pack!

She hung her head, realizing she'd left it outside.

"They seem to flourish in the cold," Annis said, motioning to the spiders. She clicked the tips of her claws together and picked one from the wall. The Sarastro gleamed in the low light. "Like me," she said and popped the baby into her mouth.

Fiona looked back at the entrance, wondering how she was going to get out of this, and saw the fuse of her Angel's Breath poking through a cobweb.

That's how.

It was on the floor, dangerously close to the cauldron. She could light the fuse on the flames and figure the rest out later. If she could get over there.

"You have to end the spell," Fiona said, standing up.

Don't look at it. Just distract her.

Her breath was shallow, but steady. Her nerves shaky, but under control. "You have to reverse it all." She tried to sound forceful, to somehow be intimidating, but only managed a hoarse whisper.

When Annis said nothing Fiona wondered if the fairy could read her mind, if she'd seen the explosive through her eyes and was just toying with her, making her think she had a chance.

"You still think I'm the bad guy, don't you?" Annis finally said, laughing. She stood and walked toward Fiona, her tattered skirts dragging across the ice, scattering spiders in her wake. Fiona noticed her skin wasn't luminous like other fairies, but pale and washed out, like the belly of a dead fish.

"I'm not the enemy, my love," Annis said, gently caressing Fiona's cheek with the tip of her claw. It was icy and sharp as any blade. "In fact, I'm going to help you."

Fiona stood very still, afraid to move. Her eyes flicked to the explosive. The baby spider was there now, draped in webs, hovering over the stick and hissing at a smaller spider that had gotten too close to his prize.

~ 169 ~

"A shame Jaydin got caught in the middle," Annis said, slowly circling Fiona, exposing her shriveled wings. "And such a handsome young thing. Just like his father. But Caelia needed to know how it feels. And now she does."

"But Lindley...," Fiona blurted without thinking.

"YOU DARE SPEAK HIS NAME TO ME?" Annis shouted. She looked down, taking a deep breath to calm herself, and Fiona saw that her hair had pulled away at the part, exposing a pale, wrinkled scalp, like it'd been wet for too long.

Fiona's eyes darted back to the cauldron. The two spiders were hissing at each other, locked in a tug of war with her Angel's Breath. The fuse danced precariously close to the licking flames.

Annis rolled the Sarastro in her hands. The flute clicked against her iron claws. "Caelia was never my friend, and she isn't yours either." She shook her head and swept toward the entrance. "She keeps a secret from you, Fiona. Did you know that?"

Fiona inched toward the left wall, desperate to reach the cauldron. She stole a glance, wondering how long until they were blown sky high by the squabbling spiders, and suddenly couldn't find them. Both spiders and the explosive were gone. She scanned the floor and saw nothing.

Come on! Where'd you go!?

"Your parents are alive," Annis said, smiling. "And she knows where they are."

Nothing could've prepared Fiona to hear such a thing. "That's a lie!" she shouted, tasting blood. She coughed, so badly she nearly lost consciousness. Instead, she lost her breath.

She fell to the floor, sprawled on her knees, gasping for air.

"She's always known they're not really dead," Annis said. She knelt beside Fiona and ran her claw lovingly over the girl's hair. "She was there. She watched them toss that cheap trinket that you wear onto the ground next to you. And she watched as they walked away because they didn't want you."

The slow stream of blood oozing from Fiona's mouth frightened her. She watched, horrified, as it thickened and began to crystallize on the ice, like the blood of a winter kill. The gentle way Annis stroked her head frightened her even more. But the old hag's words were the worst. Worse even than the blinding pain in her chest. The words pierced her heart like daggers, in its most secret, vulnerable place. She lay on the ice, twitching, unable to fight back, unable to breathe, unable even to stop listening.

"Remember that queasy feeling growing up? How it snaked through your little belly," Annis said, drawing out each word, "whispering you didn't belong? You were right. They all pretended to love you. Out of pity. But I won't pretend. I won't lie."

Fiona twisted on the ice, tormented and suffocating. Had her parents really left her alone in the world, to fend for herself? Were they out there somewhere, enjoying lives without her? Was she the only one who didn't know? She'd spent years speculating why her parents had died, why they'd all ended up in Amryn, on the banks of the Winding River that day, each scenario more heroic and tragic than the last.

What she'd never considered was that it hadn't happened at all; that they'd not been found upstream from her, cold and dead from starvation, wrapped in each other's arms, as Caelia and the Bright Eyes had explained. What she'd never considered, until now, was that they were still alive.

Her throat spasmed and she gagged. If her breath was coming back, like last time, it would have to be soon.

This is worse than before.

She tried to block the stabbing pain in her lungs, to block everything Annis was saying, but the words fell like a stinging, icy rain. Why had Caelia lied?

"My, dear, you're in a bad way," Annis said, crawling to her feet. "I wonder, have you ever thought how it must've been for Manzanita Rose? To be paired with an orphaned *human*?" She shook her head. "How disappointing for her."

Fiona's eyes flashed with anger. She may not know if her parents were dead or alive, or why they'd left her that day, but she did know her life's match. And nothing could ruin what they'd shared.

She had to fight. She had to get back to Manzy.

Her body shook, its struggle more painful than she'd thought possible, and she caught a glimpse of her hands. They'd gone numb, she realized, and her skin was a dead, ashy grey.

Because I'm not getting any air.

"*...with me,*" her mother said, "*...stay with me.*"

The voice whispered through her mind, calling her from the pain. She smiled weakly, knowing no matter what the truth was, *her* mother, the one that loved spiced mead and brushed her hair by the fire, the one that calmed her with soothing words, the one she'd created for herself and carried with her all these years, loved her very much.

As she slipped further away her thoughts became fuzzy, the pain ebbed into a dull throb, and her eyes wandered to the flames at the base of the cauldron, to the cobweb where her only chance had once been, to the glistening webs on the ceiling, their intricate patterns strangely beautiful in the eerie light. She was still now, with no strength to move anything but her eyes. She saw Annis above her, saw her lips moving and heard her muffled voice in the distance. Behind Annis was the entrance to the cave, sharp icicles hanging like jagged teeth. And outside was the night, black and cold as death's own kiss, alive somehow, moving into the cave.

Coming for me.

"You were tossed out," Annis continued, "like trash. And the rest of your life has been a lie."

Fiona's vision was blurring, the edges going black. The darkness behind Annis was closing in on them. She knew there was nothing more she could do. I should've gone for the Angel's Breath, she thought. McClane would be so disappointed. I've failed them all.

"Persephone, my love," Annis said, turning toward the entrance.

Behind Annis was the night itself, crawling toward them, answering its master's call.

I never had a chance.

Fiona lay quivering on the ice, waiting to die, waiting for the oncoming darkness to take her.

When her breath returned, inflating her battered lungs, she almost couldn't believe it. She gasped, hacking blood as she crawled to her knees, knowing she'd not survive another bout like that. She looked up and realized it wasn't the night that the fairy had summoned, but a giant Snow Spider.

It stood behind Annis, venom dripping from its fangs.

"That's more like it!" Annis said, watching Fiona struggle. She held the Sarastro in the air. "You'll like my music, just like the Neulock boy." She looked back at Persephone. "See what I've found," she said, gesturing to Fiona, "for our young ones."

Persephone hissed and scrambled toward the cauldron.

"*Your* young ones, my love," Annis said, following the giant spider. "Your young ones."

Fiona tried to stand, but was too weak.

Get up!

But she couldn't. Crawling to her knees had left her empty, like she'd spent the last two turns hauling boulders with McClane. She saw Annis holding the flute to her lips, and out of the corner of her eye she saw the baby spider scamper toward the entrance, the stick of Angel's Breath above his head. She tried to lunge, to catch him before he ran outside, but only managed to fall sideways.

"AHHH!" she cried, landing badly on her broken shoulder.

Annis stepped backward and with a sickening crunch stomped the baby, crushing it into the ice. The explosive rolled across the floor, leaving a trail of blood in its path, out of Fiona's reach and hidden in the shadows.

Persephone screeched, her cry deafening in the small cave.

"My love," Annis soothed, turning to the raging mother spider, "there are always more." She raised the Sarastro and looked back at Fiona. "Where were we?"

Fiona tried again to get up, to get away somehow, but couldn't. She lay on her side, barely breathing, too sick to stand. Her shoulder throbbed painfully with each beat of her heart. She scrunched her nose, smelling something like sulphur, but sickly sweet, like someone had smashed eggs over a freshly killed deer.

The dead baby.

She saw Annis by the cauldron, the Sarastro to her lips, and knew it was over.

When the music began Fiona had time to wonder if she would fall victim to the Carapacem Spell, like Brent, or if in her weakened state she would just die. She closed her eyes, wanting to see Manzy one last time, to hear McClane's strong voice. But there was nothing. She was alone.

The music stopped.

She opened her eyes and found Persephone holding Annis in the air by her waist. The old fairy screamed and the Sarastro fell to the floor, clattering on the ice. Persephone twisted Annis before her red eyes, then slammed her into the ceiling. Steam rose as the venom fell from Persephone's fangs, melting holes in the floor.

Fiona's heart raced. She crawled along the wall, her hands slipping on the ice as she drug herself with her one good arm toward the entrance. She'd made it only a few feet when she bumped something with her numb fingers.

My Angel's Breath!

She reached for the explosive and tried to grab it, but her fingers wouldn't work. She cupped them to her mouth and hastily blew what little breath she had over her hands. When the painful tingling began, she knew she was making progress.

She grabbed the explosive and winced. Her fingers felt like they were burning from the inside, like someone was poking her with a thousand needles. She tucked the Angel's Breath in her waistband, vowing if she got out of this she'd never take her fingers for granted again.

She looked back over her shoulder. Persephone was coming, her eyes full of hate.

And Annis was gone.

Fiona screamed, a thin, wheezy sound, and crawled as fast as she could.

Only a few more feet.

She drug herself through the shadows, along the icy floor, and felt something warm touch her leg.

"AHHH!" she cried, knowing it was Persephone, knowing the mother spider's long, hairy grip had reached her.

But when she looked, nothing but gleaming metal touched her leg.

The Sarastro!

Through the rising cloud of steam she could see Persephone closing in. She was sure if the venom touched her it would burn holes in her skin. She felt for the explosive, still tucked in her pants, and knew what she had to do.

She grabbed the Sarastro, surprised by its warmth, like it was alive in her freezing hands, and quickly traded it with the Angel's Breath. She secured the Sarastro in her waistband and grabbed the explosive. She scrambled toward the entrance, her hands and knees slipping on the ice, feeling Persephone just behind her.

Almost there.

HISS! HISS!

A fat drop of venom fell to her right, melting into the ice and splashing her arm. Her sleeve smoked and spots of it began dissolving. She could feel her arm burning as she looked up. Persephone hovered above her, the glowing red eyes malevolent and spiteful.

Fiona looked for the cauldron, for the salvation of the flames, but they were gone, squelched by the cloud of steam that had filled the cave.

From the venom.

That was all I had, Fiona thought desperately. She gritted her teeth and rolled over, determined to face her death. She was terrified, hot tears rolling down the sides of her face. With her free hand she reached for her key, clinging to an old hope, and caused the steam to shift.

Behind Persephone she saw orange. Beautiful, burning orange.

Her eyes locked on the flames. She whispered a silent prayer to the Heavens and threw the Angel's Breath hurtling toward the base of the cauldron, knowing if her plan worked she'd probably still not make it out alive.

26

Paid in Full

Morning came swiftly, the day rising under a sky so crisp and blue it held nothing but promise. Which seemed unfair, Jaydin thought, since it would be Fiona's last.

If she had to die, let it be under raging storm clouds and great crashes of thunder. He looked down and wiped the sweat from her forehead. Winds should whip through the Wood and the seas should churn. That would be more fitting, he thought. Let the songbirds be silent. Let the Heavens weep for her as I do.

She rested now, her head on his lap, the calming influence of the Moonshadow helping to ease her pain. She'd been unconscious when Ferront had found her in the early hours of the morning, cold and alone, shivering outside the remains of the cave. Had Rhiannon and Isabel not seen the explosion as they flew above, she would surely have frozen. As it was she'd lost a finger to the cold. He wrapped his palm around it again, trying to coax it back to life. For what reason he didn't know, even if it healed she would still die. It was no good anyway. The pinky finger they'd sworn so many oaths on wasn't even cold anymore, just dead. Its blackness was ugly to him, like a herald of things to come.

She'd woken only once since they'd brought her to the Wood. She'd been delirious, mumbling about Sarastros and Snow Spiders. No one knew what had happened in the mountains, least of all him. He'd been released only a short time ago, after Manzy had spoken to the King. Just when the food had started to improve, too, he thought, remembering the fresh muffin on his trencher that morning. He'd been about to enjoy it when Bo had pounded so loudly on his cell door, shouting the news of his release, that he'd dropped it, leaving nothing but scattered crumbs on the stone floor.

He'd thought the King beyond reason, that the nights of waking in a cold sweat, feeling the rough fibers of the noose scratch as it closed around his neck, would haunt him until they finally became real. But somehow Manzy had convinced the old man of the truth. Something about his daughter's finger and an ogre.

Manzy was with his mother now, standing in the reeds at the edge of the pond, still trying to figure some payment for the debt. There was no doubt in what they'd explained to him. One look at Fiona's cold, graying skin was enough to know the truth of it. She was dying. Because of him.

"Jaydin?" Fiona whispered, stirring. Her breath was ragged and irregular.

"Right here," he said, suddenly unsure of himself. The sound of her voice reminded him of all he would lose. His chest tightened. The world would be wrong without her; too dull, too *quiet*.

"Thank the Angels...you're alive! Where's Manzy?" she asked, trying to sit up.

"Not so fast," he said, easing her back down. "We're all here. But you need to rest."

She settled back down without a word.

Too easy, he thought, spreading his wings to shade her from the morning sun. She should've fought like a cat trapped in a rain barrel. "I'm worried about you," he managed.

"This is nothing," she said, laughing weakly. "Wait 'til you...see me cough. It's like walking...by the butcher's stall."

"That's not funny," he said angrily. He shook his head and looked away.

"It's a little funny," she whispered slowly. She turned her head, looking for Manzy, and winced. The bite wounds on her neck seemed to have gotten worse.

"I would've figured something out!" he shouted suddenly, his anger boiling over. He regretted it immediately, even before his mother and Manzy glanced over. He waved his hand and lowered his voice. "This is all my fault!"

"Don't try and...steal my thunder," she said through a wheezing breath. "This one is...all me." She reached for his hand and squeezed.

He wiped a tear from his face and looked back at her. Somehow her eyes still sparkled in her sunken, pale face. One more thing to lose. "You're something, Fiona Thorn. You always have been." He leaned forward and held her, hoping she knew what he'd never had the courage to say.

"Besides," she whispered, smiling at him despite her labored breathing, "you can't...be mad. I brought...a present."

He sat up and took a long, slow breath. "I have to tell you something first," he said. He had to say the words. Before it was too late.

"Me first," she demanded. "Dying girls...always get...their way." She patted her waistband, weakly searching for something, then handed him the Sarastro. "Here," she said, enjoying the surprised look on his face.

"By the Angels, Fiona! How did you get this?" he asked, taking the flute from her. He ran his fingers through his hair and looked at her, incredulous. He'd intended to throw it in the pond or the woods, or anywhere out of his sight. He'd been tricked with this flute, and the sight of it made him furious. Caelia had said some old hag with an ancient crush on his father had shaped herself into Fiona and used him to curse the Neulock boy.

Everyone kept saying he'd been a victim, that it wasn't his fault. And he knew they were right, but he couldn't get past the feeling that his music had hurt a child. Brent Neulock, a bright little soul who dreamed of the sea, was still in a catatonic state, even now, because of music that *he'd* played. No matter how many times his mother explained it, he still felt responsible. And this wretched Sarastro had been part of it. It had led to his imprisonment, to all those lonely, sweaty days when he feared for his life, and to Fiona's rash behavior, which would now be the death of her.

But when he held it in his hands, he couldn't remember why he'd been so upset.

"Annis dropped it. When the...spider got her," Fiona said. "I thought with time...you might...master it."

"I thought I'd never see it again," he said, unable to look away from its gleaming surface. The rippling water of the Moonshadow reflected on the metal. He smiled. Despite everything, he thought, it was just a flute. Perhaps he'd made too much of all that had happened. Accidents were a part of life. The important thing was that the flute belonged to him now. It was his to master, the girl had said as much. It was warm in his grip, alive somehow. He wanted to play at once, to be carried from all the sickness and death by sweet melodies, to feel the music surge through him. There was nothing else anymore, just the music.

Just like that day at the Rowan Oak.

He closed his eyes and raised the Sarastro to his lips. Nothing could be more wonderful, he thought. Nothing could be more important.

****

Fiona had known Jaydin would love the Sarastro. She'd imagined giving it to him, how the tiny scar she'd given him just above his left cheek would crinkle when he smiled, how his brown eyes would flash with amazement. Picturing the look on his face had given her something to do in the cold of the mountains, other than wonder if he and Manzy were still alive. Or how she would die. It had helped, like a crutch for a lame child.

She'd collapsed after the blast, her body bloodied and aching. She'd been too addled by the explosion to make a full account of her injuries, but as she'd lain in the snow, she'd known it was bad. She'd felt as if her insides had been beaten and bruised. She'd known men to die from the unseen damage explosions could cause. She'd smiled, alone in the dark, knowing there was a good chance she'd die that way too, or maybe from the cold. Either of those was fine by her. As long as she didn't lose her breath again.

Collapsed in the snow she'd drifted between sleep and delirium, her mind floating like a Lacewing. She'd thought of Manzy; of her fondness for oniongrass and how she smelled of warm pine after walking through the wooly rosemary that grew near the Hollow. She'd thought of their long summer rides, how the tall grasses in the meadow always tickled her toes. She'd thought of days they'd lost napping in the cool shade of their favorite Milkwood Tree, and how the velvety plush of Manzy's nose was softer than a newly born Cottonjack.

She'd wake from these fever dreams to find herself still alone, the fear of losing her breath shadowing her thoughts like a specter. Once, as she'd struggled to give her mind something to grasp, she'd seen the bright metal of the Sarastro sticking from her waistband and thought of Jaydin. Of how he would run his hand through his hair and be speechless with delight when she brought it to him.

She watched him now as he examined the flute, grateful she'd somehow lived long enough to make it happen. He looked like a child on Savior's Day morn, completely absorbed by a new toy. She was glad he liked it. She even hoped it might remind him of her after she'd gone. But to be honest, she'd not expected him to be so taken with it that he'd forget she was still here.

"Jaydin?" she said, tugging on his sleeve. This was getting ridiculous. She wasn't dead yet.

He ignored her. He didn't even seem to hear her. She remembered Kevin saying they were special, that Sarastros were more than enchanted flutes. But this was too much.

This isn't right.

She watched with growing concern as Jaydin's fingers ran along the Sarastro's smooth surface, like a miser counting his gold. The faraway look in his eye was troubling too.

What if it's still cursed? Her heart raced, suddenly fearing the worst. But with Annis gone, she reminded herself, the spells she cast would've been broken. The flute should be safe again. The music should be harmless.

Jaydin put the flute to his lips and began to play.

A cool breeze blew through the Wood, sending a shiver over Fiona's skin. She closed her eyes and tried to let the music soothe her.

But something pulled at the back of her mind, like an itch she couldn't quite reach, or a name she'd forgotten. She opened her eyes and looked for Manzy. She and Caelia were coming over now, drawn by Jaydin's music.

It's a shame Kevin isn't here, Fiona thought, he's always loved a good tune. I'd liked to have seen him again. To say goodbye. I wouldn't even have minded seeing the girls again, she thought, smiling.

The music surrounded the Moonshadow now, its lilting melody filling the warm, summer air. Maybe I'm dying, Fiona thought, for she seemed to be slipping farther and farther away and it was hard to focus. The music was so relaxing, it somehow made dying okay. But there was something that wouldn't let go. Something about Kevin, she thought, and the Sarastro. What had he said the other day?

Sarastros are more than enchanted flutes. Their magic allows the user to become one with the instrument; to bind their very soul to the flute.

Her eyes flew open. Annis hadn't been killed by Persephone, she realized.

She was in the Sarastro.

Fiona's heart pounded in her chest. She tried to sit up but couldn't. She felt more weak than she could remember, like she was paralyzed.

Like she was under a spell.

She moved her head from side to side, and thanked the Angels that she wasn't completely gone yet. She shouted for Manzy and Caelia, to tell them what was happening, but the effort cost her. Dearly.

Blood sprayed from her lips, covering the front of her tunic. It landed on her key, dotting the bronze surface with bright red.

And then, for the last time, she lost her breath.

She lay on her back, tossing her head back and forth. Her body felt trapped and heavy, like she'd been wrapped too tight in swaddling, while at the same time squeezed from the inside out.

Only her right arm could move. It twitched as she suffocated. She heard nothing but the birds chirping in the summer morning and the cursed music surrounding them. Blood ran from the side of her mouth and she watched in horror as Manzy and Caelia crumpled to the ground. The edges of her vision began to blacken. And Jaydin played on.

How could he do this? Didn't he see what was happening?

Her thoughts were muddled, like her head had been stuffed with sackcloth, and she was fading, fast. She had no air, no breath to sustain herself, and she could barely see. Yet through it all an anger burned. Had he been paying more attention to *her,* instead of that wretched flute, none of this would be happening.

She grimaced and struck out with her right arm. Jaydin was right there, still playing with his precious toy. And she wanted nothing more than to punch him.

Her aim was bad. She struck the Sarastro instead of Jaydin. It fell from his grip and landed on her blood soaked chest. She grabbed it with the only arm she could move, and threw it as hard as she could.

She heard the splash as it landed in the pond. Her vision was gone and she felt herself losing consciousness. This was how it would end. At least she'd gotten that evil thing away from Jaydin. Maybe the others still had a chance.

I should've remembered what Kevin said. I should've known about the flute.

She steadied herself, waiting for the blackness to swallow her, and wondered if her parents would be waiting, or if Annis had been right and there would be no one. She would know the truth soon.

"Fiona?" Manzy said. She nudged her head against Fiona's chest.

Fiona opened her eyes and saw her life's match standing above her, a smear of blood on her white nose. Caelia was there, too, looking down at her.

"Manzy!" she shouted. "You're bleeding!"

"Fiona," Caelia said, smiling from above, "you're breathing."

It was true. She'd been so worried about Manzy she hadn't even noticed. But she *was* breathing. Her neck still hurt, and her shoulder was aching, but she felt stronger than she had in days.

"And your color is back to normal, too," Jaydin said, shaking his head. "What's happening?"

"Annis was the life," Fiona said, taking a deep, satisfying breath. It was all becoming clear. "She was the payment." She stood up slowly, her legs still a bit shaky, and carefully walked to the edge of the Moonshadow, oblivious to the stunned looks of the others. She found nothing but sunlight dancing on the calm water. "She was in the Sarastro the whole time."

"So it's over?" Jaydin asked, looking from Fiona to his mother. "She's really going to be alright?"

"She still has need of some healing," Caelia answered, wrapping her arms around Fiona, "but I'd say it's nothing I can't handle."

"How do you feel, Fee?" Manzy asked, the blood from Fiona's chest still staining her nose. "Do you really feel better?"

"I'm think I'm fine," she said, rubbing the horse's ears. "Except for this gnawing ache," she said, pointing to her stomach, "right here."

"What is it?" Manzy asked, worried all over again. Perhaps there'd been some permanent damage caused by going so long without air, or maybe she'd suffered internal injuries from the explosion.

Fiona laughed. "I'm starving, Manzy, that's all."

"Not funny, Fiona," Manzy said, blowing through her nostrils. "Heaven's Gate."

The group walked together, surrounding Fiona protectively, as they left the Moonshadow. The Hollow wasn't far, and Caelia preferred to do her healing at home.

"Hey, Jaydin," Fiona asked, a sly smile crossing her face as they walked the path through the Wood, "what was it you were going to tell me?"

"What do you mean?" he asked.

"You know," she said, bumping into him as they walked, "earlier. You said it was *really* important. Something that couldn't wait."

Jaydin's face flushed red as a beetroot, turning the leaves of his ivy tattoo bright pink. "Oh, that!" he said, "it was nothing." He flew overhead, suddenly in a rush. "I, ah, I just remembered!" he said, looking over his shoulder as he headed into the thickness of the Wood, "we'll need thistleberry!"

"I have plenty at home," Caelia hollered, though he seemed not to have heard. He was gone before she'd even finished speaking.

"What was that about?" Manzy asked, watching him go.

"Hard to say," Fiona said, grinning. But she had a pretty good idea.

27

Ugly Anne and The Prickling Rot

"On three?" Fiona asked, her eyes bright with anticipation. Casey stood beside her, his wet fur covered in sand and his pink tongue hanging out the side of his mouth.

"Fine with me," McClane said. He winked and grabbed a stick that was resting on the edge of the fire pit. He blew on the burning end. It glowed orange in the chilly air. "One...two..."

"Wait! Wait!" Fiona shouted, looking over her shoulder at the small crowd behind her. "Dee always counts. So it's fair."

"Scared yer gonna' lose?" McClane teased, pointing his stick at her. He laughed and put it back in the fire, then grabbed the end of the fuse by her feet. It'd been strung along the beach from where they stood to a large boulder in the distance. At the other end was a pumpkin, which sat on the boulder, packed full of Blast. McClane's pumpkin was beside it, with nothing inside but his fuse and a small black disc. "Seems wet," he said, rubbing Fiona's frayed cord in his fingers. "From the mist in the air." He shrugged his shoulders. "Forfeit now and I swear to ye' no one has to know."

"No one but all of us?" Jaydin asked, laughing. Casey barked, adding his two cents.

"Yeah, Fiona," Rhiannon teased, bumping Manzy on the shoulder, "we won't tell anyone."

Fiona playfully flicked McClane's hand from her fuse, knowing full well that every bit of cord he had lying around this place was treated to resist moisture. Any demolition master worth his salt had accounted for damp fuses. Especially one that lived on the coast. His fuse was just as wet, and she knew it. He knew it, too.

"Forget it, Mick," she said, remembering the one time she had fallen for this trick. She'd been much younger then, with no experience in explosives. Just a love of watching things burn. "Not this time."

Blowing pumpkins was a fall tradition for her and McClane. And this year it had drawn a crowd. She and Manzy were leaving in the morning, heading north to the Ringing Trees, and everyone had come to wish them well. And to see the pumpkins blow.

While she and McClane had spent the day preparing their explosives, hiding from one another and secretly concocting their most volatile mixes, Delia had shown Rhiannon and Isabel how to make plum jam. They'd warmed themselves all day by the outside fire, slowly cooking the fruit in the big iron pot until it was a delicious, thick syrup. Kevin had arrived by late afternoon, just in time to watch Cricket discover her uncanny talent for apple bobbing, and to hear Foo grumble about being covered in wet satin.

Fiona grabbed her stick from the fire pit, the end alight in flame, and turned to Dee. "On three."

McClane grabbed his stick, nodded at Fiona, and waited for the count.

"Can't you two find something else to do with yourselves?" Delia said, rolling her eyes. "Something's always bursting into flames or being blown sky high around here. Someone's bound to lose another finger. And you two don't have any to spare," she scolded, glaring at McClane. "I have warm honey cakes up there, and the girls made fresh jam." She smiled at the princesses. "And," she continued, wrapping her shawl around her shoulders, "it's cold. Let's forget this nonsense and go eat."

"By the Angels, woman," McClane said, "ye' married a blastin' man! Wha'd ye expect? Posies and lace? Count a'ready!"

"Yeah, Dee," Fiona said, her chest puffed with pride, "I got him this year."

Delia pursed her lips and sighed. Despite their dangerous love of combustion she was proud of them, and their yearly foolishness. "Have it your way," she said, slowly making her way between them. She put her hands on her hips and counted. "One...Two...Three!"

The fuses were lit and the small group chattered with excitement. The white flames cracked in the chill, moist air, sparking and racing along the beach toward the pumpkins.

Casey barked and chased the burning fuses, McClane's dog through and through, then ran back and jumped at Fiona's feet.

"Pretty!" Cricket said. Her eyes flashed with mischief and she crawled to her feet, standing on Manzy's back. She pointed at the sparking fuses. "BIG! BIG!" she shouted, bouncing up and down.

"Nice try, Cricket," Rhiannon said. She looked at Isabel. "Still mad that mom made Caelia revoke her power? 'Cause that giant ball of fire would've turned us into toast."

"I guess," Isabel said, nodding. "I still think it's dumb I can only use mine in the Wood though."

"Just until the villagers become accustomed to a princess with wings, Dear," Kevin said, squinting his eyes against the blowing sand. "Your lady mother and Caelia thought it for the best."

"Speaking of the best," Fiona said, pointing down the beach, "here we go!"

The burning fuses had danced side by side along the water and were now at the base of the boulder. Halfway up Fiona's pulled ahead though, leaving McClane's sputtering in a wad of moss that clung to the side of the rock.

When the sparks from Fiona's fuse reached her pumpkin the air reverberated with a deafening sound, and the Blast-packed pumpkin exploded, sending chunks of orange rind and gooey wads of stringy insides soaring into the air.

"Impressive," Jaydin said as the last of the pumpkin guts fell to the beach. "Too bad about the moss. Looks like she did get you this year, Mick!"

McClane shot the boy a quick look, his brows drawn.

"Sir, I mean," Jaydin said. "Looks like she got you this year, Sir."

"YES!" Fiona shouted, pumping her arm in the air. "I do love the classics. Can't go wrong with Blast."

"Not so fast," McClane said, grinning. He looked back to the boulder. "We're not through yet."

The sparks from his fuse had finally fought through the damp moss and were climbing over the edge. Everyone held their breath.

But nothing happened.

"It's nothing to be ashamed of," Delia said soothingly. She put her arm around her husband and laughed. "Let the girl have her victory."

"Look!" Isabel shouted as the group began to break up. She was pointing down the beach.

Green mist had begun seeping from under the carved lid of McClane's pumpkin.

"Ha!" he said, nodding his head. "Keep a close eye, now!"

As the mist dissipated, the skin of the pumpkin began to bubble and burst. Holes opened through the sides and green slime oozed out, coating the top of the boulder. The pumpkin blistered and popped, slowly dissolving into a mushy puddle, and a noxious, rancid stink wafted over the beach.

"What's that smell?" Rhiannon cried, covering her nose. She looked around. Everyone but Cricket and McClane were doing the same. Even Foo, who was sitting on Cricket's shoulder, had buried his face in his grubby little hands.

"Wait for it, wait for it," McClane said, almost bouncing.

"It's supposed to explode, Mick," Fiona mumbled from behind her hand, "not make us gag!" Casey lay on the beach beside her, his nose under his paws.

Before McClane could respond, the air shook with a deep groaning they felt in their chests, then was sucked back down the beach with such force it made their hair dance.

McClane smiled, tucking a few loose grey strands of hair behind his ear, and counted on his thick fingers. "Watch now!"

Green flames began to burn on the remains of the pumpkin.

"...two...three!"

Right on cue a cylinder of solid green flame, wide as a small coiled rope, burst into the heavens, burning hot and strong from the top of the boulder.

Delia jumped back, bumping into Manzy. "Heaven's Gate!"

Casey stood, hiding halfway behind Fiona, and barked, his hackles raised.

Cricket squealed, watching in wonderment.

"Look at it!" Jaydin shouted. "I bet you could see it from the Wood!"

"I bet you can see it from everywhere," Isabel murmured, her head craned up at the pillar of green flame.

After a full minute, the burning green tower slowly subsided. It shrank amid the cries of the onlookers, and finally guttered out, leaving nothing but a smoking puddle of black ooze where McClane's pumpkin had been.

"Seriously?" Fiona finally said, her hands on her hips.

"That was awesome!!" Jaydin said, flying back from investigating the boulder. "BEST. YEAR. EVER."

"I thought ye'd like tha'," McClane said as Jaydin landed. "Wha's wrong, Fee? Cat got yer tongue?"

"What *was* that?" she asked, her disappointment at losing already gone. "You have to show me."

"Little a' this," he laughed, putting his arm around her as they headed up the hill, "little a' that. I call 'er Ugly Anne, after me ol' mum's sister. Mean as a snake she was, and uglier than sin."

"Boom! Boom!" Cricket shouted, sliding from Manzy's back. Foo stumbled from her shoulder and fell to the ground. He spent most of his time up there, wrapped in the satiny puffs of her sleeve, and had gotten used to her unexpected movements. But he was still hiding from the strange green fire and had been caught off guard. He shook his ugly little head and climbed to his feet.

"Am I to assume that this feral, malodorous brute has been accorded permission to remain?" Kevin asked as he slithered over the rocky ground toward Foo.

"Cricket has gotten it into her head that she's keeping him," Rhiannon said as the little ogre chased Cricket up the hill, grumbling the whole way.

McClane laughed, a deep, hearty chuckle. They'd reached the cottage and he stood by the fire, warming his hands. "Sounds like somethin' this one would'a done," he said, looking fondly at Fiona, "had we known her when she was tha' wee."

"An ogre living in the castle?" Delia asked, frowning. She pressed her finger gently on the honeycakes, testing for doneness. "Right under the Queen's nose?"

"Mom thinks he ran away," Rhiannon said, watching as Foo pulled on Cricket's dress, anxious to settle back in his spot. He was whining at her, trying to climb up to her shoulder, but kept slipping on her satiny skirts. "She doesn't know Cricket keeps him in the toad house we made last year."

Cricket leaned over and grabbed Foo. Fiona watched as he shuffled to her left shoulder. He shoved the fabric of Cricket's dress with his foot, trying to kick it out of the way, but it snagged on his ragged toenail and wrapped around him. He flung his arms wildly and got free, then head-butted the fabric angrily. He grabbed the puff, about to rip it to pieces, but rubbed it against his wrinkled face instead. His tiny mouth curved in an unlikely smile. He nestled himself into the poof above her left shoulder, so the wispy bottoms of Cricket's hair tickled the top of his bald head, and began to purr.

Delia clucked in disapproval. She snapped a blanket in the air, shaking the loose ashes from it, and laid it beside the kettle. "Not sure how I feel about that, girls," she said, giving them a hard look as she shook out the rest of the blankets.

"The ugly little beast must be good comp'ny for her," McClane said, settling himself on a blanket. Casey ambled over, a sandy tangle of pumpkin guts hanging from his mouth, and settled by the old man.

Cricket smiled and patted Foo, then started skipping around the fire, weaving in and out of everyone else.

"That reminds me," Rhiannon said, "Fiona never told me how you guys met."

"Bet she din't," McClane said. He looked at Delia and winked, his blue eyes full of fond memories. "Just a bit of a thing she was, skinny as a willow branch, though not so yielding." He grinned and nodded as Cricket went by. "A few years older than your little sister I'd wager, when I found her. Standin' outside of me old barn, she was, just watchin' it burn. Mesmerized by the flame. She's got fire in her blood. Always has," he finished proudly, "least since I've known her."

Fiona rolled her eyes and tucked her knees under her chin. Jaydin laughed and nudged her on the shoulder. "It was an accident, we know. Just like the chickens."

"You burnt it down?" Rhiannon asked, stunned. "The one down by the shore?"

"Yeah," Fiona said, hiding her head in her knees. She wasn't proud of it, but it was true. She'd been wandering alone that day, knocking down the tall grass with a birch switch, and stumbled on McClane. She'd sat in the woods, just beyond the clearing above the cottage, and watched, captivated by the big man and how he made things explode with such fury. As soon as he'd gone in the little house, she'd snuck in the barn to give it a try.

"How old were you?" Isabel asked.

"About six," Delia said, smiling. She stirred the jam, then heaped a few spoonfuls into a jar.

"After I found her tha' day," McClane said, "Dee and I just figured it was safer, for everyone really, to take her in from time to time." He picked a small piece of charred wood from the ground and tossed it at Fiona. She looked up from her knees and he smiled, his blue eyes twinkling. "Turns out I was right. She's not burned a barn since."

Fiona smiled, a sly grin that put one in mind of secrets told in dark alleys, and raised her eyebrows at McClane.

"Have ye'?" he asked, surprised.

"No," she laughed, taking the jar of jam from Delia. The outside was sticky with spilled syrup. She held her hand down and Casey licked her fingers clean.

"I don't know what to say," Rhiannon said. She was looking at Fiona with something between admiration and disgust, like she'd just been given an adorable puppy to hold and suddenly realized it was a timber wolf instead.

"She was always a handful," McClane went on, beaming with pride. "Still is. But worth it." He leaned back on his elbows. "I s'pose she wouldn't a' told you about the year I spent teachin' her to use Angel's Breath either, huh?"

"That was a time I'd sooner forget," Jaydin said, rolling his eyes.

"Okay," Delia cut in, "that's enough for now, boys." She shushed them, waving her hands in front of her. "Find something else to do, now, other than pick at my girl."

McClane shrugged his shoulders and winked at Fiona. "Where's the food ya been talkin' bout, Dee? There's an angry badger tearin' at me insides."

Delia passed the cakes around the hungry group. Cricket had no sooner reached for hers than Foo ran down the little girl's arm, headfirst for the sweet, and stuck one of his tusks in her pudgy little finger, knocking the cake to the ground. Before Delia could say a word, Cricket had the ogre hung up by the back of his pink dress on a hook above the fire.

"Bad!" she shouted, sucking on her bleeding finger.

Good thing the little monster's so small, Fiona thought. He'd need a firm hand. She reached for a honeycake and the sweet, sugary smell made her realize how glad she was to be here. Delia had a way with food. It was one of the things that'd kept her coming back when she was little. "Anyway," she said sarcastically, gesturing toward Cricket, who was still sucking on her bleeding finger, "the ogre seems harmless enough."

"As if," Rhiannon said, rolling her eyes.

"And Cricket obviously loves him," Fiona continued, pointing to where he'd been hung, dangerously close to the fire.

Foo squirmed and ran his legs in the air. "ARRGHH! ARRGHH!" he shouted, pulling his legs up under him. He looked like an ugly little doll about to melt.

~ 192 ~

"Is that what you'd call it?" Jaydin asked, getting up to move Foo. He patiently showed Cricket where the fire had started to singe the hem of the ogre's dress and explained that he couldn't be that close to the flame. Cricket nodded and hugged the nasty beast to her chest. She fluffed his damp dress, which had probably saved his life, looked him over to make sure he wasn't hurt, then took the ribbon from her hair and tied him like a pig on a spit to the handle of the kettle, much farther from the flame.

"Stay," she said, giving him a look that meant business. She turned to Delia, took the fresh piece of cake that was being offered, and sat politely beside her sisters to enjoy it.

"That's exactly what I'd call it," Fiona said, smiling at Jaydin in the evening firelight. "Love."

The fire was warm and relaxing, lulling them with its soothing blaze. Even Delia stopped bustling and found a spot beside McClane. They sat, content to lazily watch the flames and enjoy the good food after a day full of excitement. Jaydin pulled his lute from behind him and started to play. Fiona watched his fingers gently pick on the strings. The fire snapped and soft music filled the air.

She would miss him. She smiled, remembering when he'd surprised her with the lodestone cuff. She'd been depressed about losing her power. She'd just come from a long, discouraging morning at the Hollow, trying to coax her levitation to the surface. Caelia had finally concluded that she must've come so close to death during her ordeal in the mountains that the magic could no longer sustain itself. Having nothing substantial to bind to it'd fled her body like a soul departing for the heavens.

She'd run into Jaydin on her way out. The thought of losing the only magical power she'd ever been given had her in a foul temper. He'd followed alongside as she'd stomped through the Wood. She'd been about to tell him to leave, to just leave her alone, when he'd smiled, that scar above his left cheek crinkling perfectly, and handed her the package. He'd bundled it so clumsily in burlap it'd looked about the size of a melon. But it had brightened her spirits.

How he'd managed to sneak her lodestone star out of her pack and have it made into an earcuff was anyone's guess. But she'd been wearing it ever since.

The King had given her the star in honor of her service to Brent and the girls. A rare piece of white lodestone, small and vaguely star shaped, it was revered for its magnetic properties. He'd presented it to her at the banquet, days after returning from the mountains.

The atmosphere had been so charged that day, she remembered, full of an exuberant energy that had reminded her of Foster's Shine. Fairies had flitted in the air and lounged in trees like bright sparkling jewels. Bright Eyes of all kinds had wandered the castle grounds too, having made the journey from the Dappled Forest. She'd even seen Boswell, the old eagle who'd taken her into his nest so many years ago.

Just before the feast she'd stood with the King, in front of everyone, under the flowing banners that had decorated the Great Stairs. She'd been unsettled, unsure of her emotions. He'd already absolved her and Jaydin of any wrong doing or crime. She'd known she should be grateful. But it'd been hard to forget how eager he'd been to believe in their guilt. And he was always so pompous.

He'd presented her before all of Amryn. "Fiona Thorn," he'd said, his regal accent and haughty demeanor grating on her nerves even as he'd honored her, "as true and bright a friend as any of the stars above." He'd placed the lodestone in the palm of her hand and whispered, "May this bring you good luck and blessings always."

It had seemed too good to be real. Yet as she'd looked over the vast crowd, she couldn't help but wonder if her parents were there. If they'd stood amongst the feasting tables, secretly proud as the King honored her. Were they full of regret for leaving her, or happy to be rid of her? Surely neither, she'd thought, scolding herself for foolishness as she'd scanned one last time and walked down the Stairs. Annis was the liar, not Caelia. Her parents were dead.

She glanced at Jaydin in the firelight, at his beautiful fingers, how he played with such heart, and sighed. She still couldn't believe any of it had worked.

She looked around the fire. Dee was propped against McClane's big chest, his arm around her and his deep voice humming along to Jaydin's lute. Cricket had untied Foo from the kettle and was tearing some cake into pieces for him. He'd somehow already covered himself in plum jam. He sat on her shoulder, licking the sweet syrup from his hairy arms. Isabel sat beside them, cross legged, next to Rhiannon, with Kevin nestled in her lap. Casey was pressed against Jaydin, and Manzy stood behind them all, nibbling on what little grass she could find.

We won't be gone long, Fiona thought, already missing everyone. The only way she'd gotten Manzy to agree to the trip at all was to promise to keep it short. Which was fine. She was feeling better, some good rest and Caelia's healing had done wonders, but her shoulder still ached at night. And she'd had enough of snow to last a long while.

She looked at the dark tip of her little finger, still dead from the cold. Most of the finger had healed, but Caelia had said the tip was gone. Fiona had finally grown used to its numbness, how it didn't have any sensation at all, like it had been carved from a piece of wood.

We'll be home in a few weeks, she thought, looking at Jaydin. Definitely before the first frost. But still, she would miss him. A shame he couldn't come too, she thought. Lindley might still be there. And Jaydin hadn't seen his father in more than a year. But being Guardian came first.

"Excellent!" Manzy said, pawing her front foot in the dirt as Jaydin finished. A haze of dust clung to her leg. "That was wonderful."

Jaydin smiled and took a small bow.

"Fiona," McClane said, reaching for another cake. His hand made it look like a nut in a bear's paw. "I ran inta' Bo in the village."

A hush settled over the group and everyone looked furtively at Jaydin. No one had spoken of his imprisonment in weeks.

"It's alright," he said, taking a deep breath, "Bo was actually pretty nice." He nodded at McClane. "I can see why you two are friends."

"Said the same 'bout you," McClane chuckled. "If yer gonna' be locked up," he said, nodding, "Bo's the jailor ye'd want."

"Anyway," Delia interrupted. She stood and wrapped her arm around Jaydin protectively. "All that's over now." She patted his arm and handed him another cake, dripping with extra jam. "Why would you mention such a thing, Mick?"

"I was gettin' to it," he said with a mouthful of cake, "if yer all done sissyin' over the boy." He widened his eyes at his wife. "Don't look at me like tha', either, he's nearly a man grown, with time served."

Fiona laughed as McClane wiped his mouth with the back of his hand. She couldn't decide what was funnier—McClane just being himself or the idea that Jaydin was almost a man.

"Brandywine's gone and snatched his nephew ta' work in the kitchens. Bo says the boy's crazy for food and the like. But it leaves him short." He looked at Fiona from across the fire. "He thought maybe ye'd want the spot."

"As a jailor?" Manzy asked, lifting her head from the grass.

"I think she'd be perfect," Rhiannon said, snickering.

"It might come in handy," Jaydin said, nudging Fiona with the tip of his outstretched wing, "having someone on the inside."

She rolled her eyes. "A bit late, don't you think?" She rubbed her chin, pretending to consider it. "Having access to Graven and his two slugs does make it tempting though." She stretched her legs out and smirked. "But I think I'll pass."

"I told him as much," McClane said. "Sides, yer trip north is in the way."

A silence hung in the evening air, their minds filled with memories; how this summer had ended so differently from all the rest, how some of them had nearly lost everything.

Rhiannon hugged Isabel as the young girl wiped a tear from her face, remembering Winkle. Kevin slid just a little closer to Cricket, reminding himself that despite her fascination with the offensive little ogre, they were a team. She loved him. And when the time was right, provided her parents had no objections, he would begin to train her in the honorable ways of espionage. McClane and Delia exchanged a look, in the way that old married couples do, knowing how frightfully close they'd come to losing the only child they'd ever shared. And Fiona reached up, gently caressing Manzy's velvet nose, then leaned on Jaydin's shoulder.

They were quiet for some time, staring into the fire.

"Dad said Graven isn't to be brought out of the dungeon cell for any reason," Isabel said, her voice hushed, "even on Savior's Day."

"And good riddance," Delia said. She turned her head and spit over her shoulder.

"The other two aren't farin' so well, either," McClane said, a smile peeking from the corner of his mouth. "They've come down wit' the Prickling Rot."

"Really?" Isabel asked, her eyes wide.

"I didn't know it was real!" Rhiannon said, grimacing.

Fiona's mouth dropped. Prickling Rot was rare, but very real. Caused by ingesting the fungus that grew on the underside leaves of the Baneberry bush, the Rot started as a simple rash; small but very itchy, much like Poison Oak. Once scratched open though the sores began to ooze an acidic mucus, burning the skin as it spread. And spread it did. It was almost impossible to get rid of, too. The victim had nothing much to look forward to but years of burning itching and scratching, covered in seeping, crusting sores.

The Rot was famous with little children mostly, an ailment threatened by tired mothers with thin mouths who'd had enough foolishness. *"Put that down or you'll get the Rot!"* was commonly heard throughout the village. And though Fiona had never had the benefit of a tired mother's threats, she had been lucky enough to know Chiery, a flickerfawn she used to play hide and seek with who'd taught her that while Baneberry was one of *her* favorite treats, for all other creatures it was poison, causing the Prickling Rot.

Fiona smiled and started to giggle. Nobody deserved it more, she thought. She could just see them, Wilkes hunched in a corner of his sweaty cell, moaning and cursing as he scratched, undoubtedly blaming the whole thing on Cal. And Cal rubbing his lanky, ugly self against the rough stone walls, trying to scratch a spot he just couldn't reach, whining the whole time, not knowing what to do without his creepy little partner to bark orders.

They must've gotten it from eating that poor flickerfawn, she thought, sighing. Serves them right.

"Has anyone had word of Brent?" Manzy asked, hoping to change the subject to something less vile. "Fiona and I haven't seen him since the banquet."

"He's fine," Delia said, laughing. "I took some mending to his mother the other day and he was on her heels for licorice string and sour suckers the whole time. We could barely get a word in with all his nagging." She shook her head and exhaled deeply. "Poor child. To think what he went through."

"I don't feel bad for him anymore," Isabel said. "He runs around the castle bailey after lessons scaring the little ones with stories of how it felt to be bewitched. He made Lottie Bates cry."

Rhiannon snickered and stood. "Mom will make *us* cry if we don't head home soon." She nudged Isabel's shoulder. "Come on. It's already dark. And Prince is hungry."

Isabel huffed, but gathered Cricket and said her goodbyes.

"Don't forget," Delia said, hugging Isabel, "you're all welcome, even if Fiona isn't here." She leaned over, making sure Foo wasn't too close, and kissed Cricket on the cheek. "I mean it," she said.

"Thank you," Rhiannon said. "And thanks for the cooking lesson." She gestured to the box she held, filled with jars of plum jam that Delia insisted they take.

Fiona walked them to the barn with Kevin sliding along in the dirt. He'd decided to see the girls home, since it had gotten so dark. Prince Alex was waiting in a large stall, casually working his way through a pile of hay that Rhiannon had given him earlier.

"He's a good looking horse," Fiona said, looking at Prince. "A bit well bred for my taste, but a fine one to have at your side." She smiled and hoped the girl understood. "He could've come out with us you know, instead of being in here all day. No one would've minded."

"As soon as I told him there were going to be explosions," Rhiannon said, bringing him out of the stall, "he told me he wanted to stay here." She ran her hand over his smooth neck and smiled. "He hates loud noises."

"My understanding was that Caelia nullified your gift of the Iomlan Tongue," Kevin said from outside the barn. He was keeping his distance, out of respect for Prince Alex. He knew how much horses hated snakes.

"She did," Rhiannon said, tightening the girth of her saddle. "I asked her to. I couldn't take all the chatter in my head." She smiled and hopped up. The leather of her saddle creaked pleasantly and she arranged her skirts. "But we agreed I should still be able to talk to Prince." She leaned forward and hugged him, then sat up and nodded.

"He sees you, you know," she continued, gesturing to Kevin. "He says he remembers you from before." She laughed and tapped Isabel's shoulder with her foot. "Prince says it was Kevin that day on the Plains."

Isabel looked confused. "What day?"

"I knew it!" Fiona said, clapping her hands. "I thought it was weird you showed up right after that!"

"What are we talking about?" Isabel asked. She slumped her shoulders and huffed. "How come I never know what's going on?"

Kevin slid slowly into the barn, keeping an eye on Prince. The horse looked calm, but it was his experience that a frightened horse could stomp a snake, even a trained professional like him, into bloody bits before anyone knew what had happened.

He stopped in front of Isabel and raised himself up, balancing on his lower half, until he was almost as tall as her waist. "I owe you an apology," he said. His gold eyes met Isabel's. "I was the one who ran in front of Midnight." He looked down, blinking his big lashes. "I was the cause of your fall that day on the Plains."

"Is that all?" Isabel said. She leaned over and kissed the top of his smooth, black head. "Consider yourself forgiven." She smiled, took a big step back and whispered *Glissadia Ascenti* so softly they barely heard her. Flame red wings sprouted under her arms.

"Come on," she said, holding her arm out for Kevin. "You can ride with me."

He looked at her wings and shook his head. "This is not in compliance with your arrangement. I cannot be complicit in this." And then, because he was nervous, he sneezed. "ACHOOO!" His body stiffened and shot out, straight as a board.

"AKE! AKE!" Cricket cried, running from outside the barn. She laughed and plopped in the dirt beside him. Foo grumbled from her shoulder, growled at all of them, opening his mouth in what would've been a most ferocious way were he not the size of a baby chipmunk, and readjusted himself in her sleeve poof.

"No one will see her," Rhiannon said, heading out of the barn on Prince. "It's dark as a raven out here. Besides," she said, "she does it all the time."

"By the Angels," Kevin said, turning to Fiona. She was leaning against a stack of hay bales, chewing on the side of her fingernail. "This is your doing. Your influence is, well, troubling."

She shrugged her shoulders. "Tell it to the judge, Ebeneezer. I can't help it if they have good taste."

"This is highly inappropriate, I tell you," he said, ignoring Rhiannon and Fiona's giggling. He snaked his way up Isabel's body until he was wrapped around her shoulders. "Though it does accord one a more desirable vista than traveling beneath frills and frocks."

Fiona helped Cricket into her saddle pouch, making sure her skirts didn't bunch uncomfortably, and nodded. "See you all soon."

"Have a great trip," Rhiannon said. "And stay out of trouble." She waved and headed up the path toward the woods. Isabel and Kevin followed close behind, soaring through the night sky.

Manzy and Jaydin met Fiona as she walked down the hill toward the fire.

"Are you leaving too?" she asked, leaning into Jaydin.

"Not 'til morning," he said. He smiled at Manzy, exchanging a look with the Bright Eye. "I like to start big trips at sunrise."

"What are you talking about?" Fiona asked. She stopped, her hands on her hips. "What are you two up to?"

"I'm finally free," Jaydin said, hovering just above the ground. "I'm not Guardian anymore." He watched Fiona, waiting for a reaction. He and Manzy had planned this surprise for weeks. Everyone had known, even McClane and Delia.

"What?" Fiona asked.

"Isabel and Sebille Shimmerfrost are Guardians now, not me," he said, swooping joyously in a loop. "I'm going with you to the Ringing Trees!" He landed in front of her and tilted his head. "Unless you don't want me to."

Fiona smiled so widely she gave thanks to the Angels it was dark. There was no need for him to know how happy this made her. Her heart fluttered, making it a little hard to breathe. He could finally come along and be part of the adventure, instead of just hearing about it after they'd come home.

Her mind raced with the possibilities. There was no way she'd sleep tonight. He could play for them each night, even by day if he felt like it. They would hear the Trees for the first time together. Kevin had said they were most melodic in the fall, too. She couldn't wait to see Jaydin's face. And if they found Lindley! This was the best news she'd had since the debt had been paid at the Moonshadow.

"Whatever," she said, coughing into her hand. It was the only thing she could do to hide her beaming smile. "The north is no joke." She headed for the fire, desperate to get away until she could control herself again, but he followed right beside.

"Get some sleep," she said, and despite her better judgement, she smiled at him. He was floating there, so eager and beautiful, she couldn't help herself. "We camp hard, too," she added, "so put your big girl pants on." She punched him in the arm, ignoring Manzy's snickering from behind. "And no whining, either. I hate whining."

Manzy trotted forward, wedging between them. "Let's just try not to blow one of the kingdom's great wonders off the map while we're there."

"We'll see," Fiona said, remembering the handful of little black discs McClane had slipped in her pack, each stamped with **UA** in bright green. "We'll see.